STEALTH OF THE NINJA

OTHER BOOKS BY
PHILIP ROY

The Kingdom of No Worries (2017)

Mouse Vacation (2016)

Mouse Pet (2015)

Eco Warrior (2015)

Jellybean Mouse (2014)

Mouse Tales (2014)

Me & Mr. Bell (2013)

Seas of South Africa (2013)

Frères de sang à Louisbourg (2013)

Blood Brothers in Louisbourg (2012)

Outlaw in India (2012)

Ghosts of the Pacific (2011)

River Odyssey (2010)

Journey to Atlantis (2009)

Submarine Outlaw (2008)

Stealth
of the Ninja

Philip Roy

RONSDALE PRESS

STEALTH OF THE NINJA
Copyright © 2017 Philip Roy

RONSDALE PRESS
3350 West 21st Avenue, Vancouver, B.C., Canada V6S 1G7
www.ronsdalepress.com

Typesetting: Julie Cochrane, in Minion 12 pt on 16
Cover Art & Design: Nancy de Brouwer, Massive Graphic Design
Paper: Ancient Forest Friendly "Silva" (FSC)—100% post-consumer waste,
    totally chlorine-free and acid-free

Ronsdale Press wishes to thank the following for their support of its publishing
program: the Canada Council for the Arts, the Government of Canada through the
Canada Book Fund, the British Columbia Arts Council, and the Province of British
Columbia through the British Columbia Book Publishing Tax Credit program.

 Canada Council Conseil des arts
for the Arts du Canada
 Canadä
 BRITISH COLUMBIA
ARTS COUNCIL
An agency of the Province of British Columbia

Library and Archives Canada Cataloguing in Publication
Roy, Philip, 1960–, author
    Stealth of the ninja / Philip Roy.

(The submarine outlaw series; 8)
Issued in print and electronic formats.
ISBN 978-1-55380-490-1 (softcover)
ISBN 978-1-55380-491-8 (ebook) / ISBN 978-1-55380-492-5 (pdf)

    I. Title. II. Series: Roy, Philip, 1960– . Submarine outlaw series; 8.

PS8635.O91144S74 2017   jC813'.6   C2017-901133-2   C2017-901134-0

At Ronsdale Press we are committed to protecting the environment. To this end we
are working with Canopy and printers to phase out our use of paper produced from
ancient forests. This book is one step towards that goal.

Printed in Canada by Marquis Printing, Quebec

for Leila

ACKNOWLEDGEMENTS

Once again I would like to thank Ron and Veronica Hatch for their continued guidance in the creation of this series. I always strive to do my best, but they continue to show me *how* to do my best. Thanks also to Meagan and Julie, and everyone else at Ronsdale. A special thanks to my dear wife Leila, to whom this book is dedicated, and without whose love and steadfast support it simply would not have been written. Thanks to all my wonderful kids: Julia, Petra, Thomas, Julian, and Eva, who inspire me constantly to reach higher. Thanks to my wonderful mom Ellen for her undying love and open ear, and to my sister Angela, for her wonderful spirit and generous heart. Thanks to my great friends, Chris, Natasha, and Chiara, and also to the many readers of the series, especially those who take the time to share their ideas with me. Lastly, thanks to the teachers and librarians who invite me to speak with students in the schools. It remains by far my favourite part of being an author.

"*Ninjutsu concerns two ends, namely life and death.
To be able to destroy but also have the capacity to
cure—life and death are intimate aspects of the essence
of ninjutsu, because it concerns survival.*"

— DR. KACEM ZOUGHARI,
The Ninja: Ancient Shadow Warriors of Japan

Chapter One

∽

THERE ARE PLACES in the world where the sea flows in gigantic wide circles, like slowly spinning merry-go-rounds. You will find the strangest things drifting on the surface there, or just beneath it: messages in bottles, spiders in coffee cups; sea buoys, sea mines, fishing nets, fishing lines; living things, dead things, and plastic—endless, unsinkable, indestructible plastic.

Most of it is just thrown into the sea, or dumped from ships, or carried down rivers, but sometimes the sea reaches up and takes it, along with boats, cottages, animals, and people. All of this stuff drifts around and around until it collides with a passing ship, or a whale, or becomes waterlogged and sinks. But some of it, especially the plastic, will float forever.

Plastic never becomes part of the sea. Fish eat it, sharks eat it, whales, turtles, dolphins, and seabirds eat it. And it kills them. Then, when their bodies decompose, or get torn apart by other creatures, the plastic re-emerges to float on the sea again. Imagine if you swallowed Lego pieces when you were three years old, and they were still in your stomach when you were ninety. And a thousand years later, when archeologists stumbled upon your grave and picked through your bones . . . they found Lego.

I dream of a ship that gobbles plastic the way minesweepers picked up sea mines during the wars. I dream of it every day as I watch the plastic drift by. I know that the sea is dying. I mean, the water will always be there, of course, but the life in it won't. And even though there are still days when whales breach in front of my sub, and dolphins race playfully past, and flying fish soar over my head with the funny whispering of their fins, there are much longer stretches when I see nothing on the water but garbage and torn nets with rotting sea animals, as if the sea were nothing but one humongous human garbage patch.

Recently, about six hundred miles southeast of Japan, I met a remarkable man who was doing what I want to do— cleaning up the plastic. He was an odd sailor for sure—very old and very ingenious, and his story is bizarre to tell. And yet, in the oddest way, he has filled me with new hope for the sea.

⁖

I saw her for the first time through the periscope. From her markings I could tell she was a small freighter out of East Asia, with a sharp pointy bow and pointy stern, but she sagged in the middle like a deep-sea fishing trawler. She was reddened with rust, and as the late sun fell down on her, she looked almost more like a painting than a ship on the sea. As we drew near, I wondered if she had been abandoned. There were no lights, no flags, no visible cargo or people on board, and she was drifting sideways in the current. Barnacles and sea coral had grown into a grotesque skirt three feet wide at her waterline. She looked as if she had been dragged up from the bottom of the sea.

I circled her twice, cried "Ahoy!" half a dozen times, and banged on her crimson hull with a gaff. Half an hour later I threw a rope onto her deck. It took four tries to hook it. I tied one end to a handle on the portal and moored the sub. Then, with a flashlight in my pocket, I shinnied my way up the rope and climbed onto her deck.

Ships are like people in a way: they die young or they die old. They might get sick, or damaged, or even filled with holes, but still sail for a while if the sea decides that's how it's going to be. If this ship was truly abandoned, then by the law of the sea I had the right to claim her. I could tie a rope to her bow and tow her away, except that . . . there was nowhere to go.

It would be impossible anyway. The barnacle skirt made

her a dead weight to tow. And my sub was tiny in comparison. She was probably two hundred and fifty feet long. My sub was twenty-five. It would be like a minnow towing a whale.

And what would I do with her if I could take her? She was just a shell of her former self; I knew that the moment I stepped aboard and began to explore. I could feel it and smell it—the smell of metal that has lost its strength.

Oddly, I had a strong sense of being watched. I kept turning my head, expecting to find someone behind me. But I scoured every inch of her and never found so much as an empty can of beans. If there were somebody here, I would have seen a sign of it, something. Yet every time I turned a corner into a passageway, or climbed a ladder, or poked my head into a cabin; and every time I found myself back on deck, I felt someone's eyes on me.

And there were suspicious smells. On the deck in my rubber sneakers I'd smell the usual odours of an old ship: rust, salt, rope, and tar. But then, when I wasn't thinking about it, I'd catch the scent of grilled fish, onions, garlic, and tomatoes. I'd look around and try to follow those smells, but they would disappear as soon as I turned a corner.

And there were sounds. The wind blew across the bow, lifted a metal flap on the bridge, and dropped it against the steel wall. But that was a predictable sound, the kind you stop hearing after a while, even though it clangs like a bell. Down in the engine room, where the only light was the light of my flashlight, and where I had to brush spiderwebs out of my hair because spiders in this part of the world can be poisonous, the hull creaked and moaned like cows in a barn.

But those were identifiable sounds. What spooked me were the smaller, sharper sounds, like a dropped wrench, or a tin can kicked by a foot. Those were the sounds I couldn't identify, and they always came from the opposite end of the ship, and sounded as though they were caused by someone.

And then I heard something that stopped me dead in my tracks: someone laughing. It sounded like a girl, but it was thin and far away. I heard it as clearly as my own breath, and yet I wondered if it could have been the wind, except that I had never heard the wind sound like that before. It echoed through the halls and walls of the ship and curled my toes in my sneakers.

And then there were shadows: the ones created by my flashlight, and the ones that appeared out of nowhere. They spooked me at least half a dozen times, but were probably caused by my movement through the ship. There simply was no one here.

I had seen so many things drift on the sea in two and a half years, but I had never seen a whole ship rusted out so badly, and so full of dents and holes that she should have settled on the bottom long before I was born. Here she was sitting on the water like a turtle on its back, as red as an apple, as lonely as the wind that stuck to her. Never had I seen a ship that looked and sounded so much like a living creature.

I spent three hours exploring every inch of her, except for

the holds. They were rusted shut. But they must have been empty, because they had sounded hollow when I banged on the ship's side with the gaff. And the ship wasn't sitting low in the water; she was about midway, which was probably only because she was carrying water. Why she hadn't sunk yet was a mystery to me.

At first hint of twilight, I shinnied down the rope, swung it free from the deck, climbed into the sub, and motored away.

Half a mile north, I took a quick peek through the periscope. I wanted to see her one last time before the sun went down. Already her redness had faded to brown. Darkness was about to engulf her. There, standing on the bow as if he were standing on top of the world, was an old man watching us sail away.

Chapter Two

∽

NIGHT FELL. I didn't want to return to the ship in the dark. Neither did I want to leave. Normally I'd dive to a hundred feet, shut everything off and go to sleep. But I couldn't do that or the ship would drift away in the night, and I might not see her again. I needed to find out what the old man was doing on her.

And so, about a quarter of a mile away, I sealed the hatch— far enough away from the ship that we wouldn't bang into each other, but close enough that we would drift in the same current. It was extremely unlikely anything would run into us during the night. Any other ship would pick us up on radar and veer away to avoid a collision. Still, I left the radar on, trusting that its beeping would wake me. I was a pretty light sleeper.

I shut everything else off, shared a snack with Hollie and Seaweed, my dog and seagull crew, climbed into bed, and closed my eyes. But it was hard to sleep. I drifted in and out of dreams that the old man was a ghost. In the middle of the night I was sure of it, and it gave me chills knowing that all the time I had explored the ship he had been watching me. When the morning sun brightened the window in the floor of the sub and flashed flecks of gold through the surface, I decided to moor to the ship again, climb the rope, and find the old man.

This time I considered carrying the gaff. What if the old man was crazy? What if he attacked me? I'd be safer if I carried a weapon.

I thought about it while I ate a pot of porridge and drank a cup of tea. Hollie and Seaweed shared dog biscuits and water. They ate quickly and then stared at me as if they were starving. Nobody can watch you eat like a seagull and a dog.

In the end, I decided against carrying a weapon. I was turning seventeen in a few days, and pretty strong. What chance would an old man stand against me?

Seaweed came out of the portal while I climbed the rope and flew to the top of the bridge. That was good because I knew that if he saw so much as a mosquito twitch, he would squawk his head off. Seaweed was extremely attentive and probably the toughest seagull that ever lived. He could be absolutely ferocious on occasion, especially to crabs, which he liked to rip apart for fun and eat. Hollie was the opposite. He liked everybody and didn't have an aggressive bone in his body.

As soon as I stepped onto the deck, I knew I was being watched. I could feel it in my bones. There was somebody here for sure, hiding in the shadows. I pretended I didn't know and went down the deck as if I didn't have a care in the world, whistling a song to show that I thought I was alone.

But it didn't make any difference. I walked the entire ship again and found nothing. There was nobody here, unless they were inside the holds. And that didn't seem possible.

Then I wondered, was I just trying too slowly? What if I moved faster: would I catch the old man in the act of running from place to place? I would surely be faster than him, so perhaps that was all I needed to do—run around the ship as fast as I could, and catch him in the act.

So I tried.

I crouched down behind a railing on the stern and counted to a hundred in my head. Then, I burst from behind the railing, bolted down the starboard side of the deck, turned around, and bolted back on the port side. But my sneaker caught on the edge of a metal plate, and I went headfirst onto the deck, rolled a few times, and banged into the stern railing. It hurt so much that I cried out. I raised my head and scanned the bridge. Seaweed was still sitting on top, quietly watching me. He must have thought I was nuts.

Obviously the old man was not on deck. So I went inside, rubbing my shoulder, and ran around as quickly as I could, which wasn't easy. In the first place, it was dark, and the doorway between each room rose a foot above the floor, so I had to jump over them. Then there were ladders between the floors, and going up and down them as quickly as I could didn't take long to exhaust me. "This is ridiculous!" I said to myself, bending over to catch my breath. "There's no one here!" If there were, I would have found him. There was no way an old man could outrun me.

Down in the engine room it was too dark to run around, and the walkway was just an iron platform raised above the floor, which made it easy to trip and fall. I crept through as quietly as I could, listening to the strange moaning of the hull. And then I felt the gentle tap of a finger come down on my shoulder. I yelled, jumped out of the way, and spun around. There wasn't anything there. I pointed my flashlight, but all I saw were shadows dancing on the walls. Then I felt the finger on my shoulder again, and I bolted out of there as fast as I could go, banging into the walls on my way.

Back out on deck, I was sweaty, bruised, and seriously spooked. I had been touched by somebody, or *something*, and yet hadn't seen a single thing. An old man couldn't outrun me, hide from me, and tap my shoulder without my even seeing him, unless there was something supernatural about him. And that was unnerving. Before going back inside, or looking any further, I decided to get some water from the sub. I was dying of thirst and wanted to check on Hollie. The moment I took a step towards the rope, Seaweed started squawking loudly. I turned my head to look up at him, and nearly jumped two feet off the ground. The old man was right behind me.

I jumped so high, and made such a frightened shout, the old man bent over in laughter, and his laugh was high-pitched, like a girl's.

He was a small man, but his hands were large and rough, like bear claws. He reminded me of my grandfather in that way, except that he didn't look like a fisherman. His eyes were glassy like the fishermen who spent their lives on the water and grew an extra protective film over their eyes, like seals, but he looked more like a monk, or a priest. His face was gentle, kind, and wise. It was cut with laugh wrinkles, which meant he had probably spent most of his life laughing. And yet there was something about him that was sad, as if he carried happiness on the outside, but sadness on the inside.

"Hello," I said.

He smiled, but didn't answer. I didn't know if he spoke English.

"Is this your ship?"

He nodded. Now I knew that he could.

I didn't want to be nosy but couldn't help asking, "Why are you here?"

"Why am I here?" he repeated. He looked down at his feet,

and his brow furrowed into a thoughtful expression. But he never answered the question, and I think his mind drifted somewhere else before he could. Or maybe he never intended to. He pointed to the sea behind me, and opened his eyes wide. Curious, I turned around to look. I didn't see anything but water. When I turned back . . . he was gone.

What the heck? Was I seeing things? Was my mind playing tricks on me? I didn't think so. I didn't feel any different. I mean, I *was* more tired lately, but was I seeing things that weren't really there? Was I starting to lose my mind?

Nope. When I looked up, I saw the old man staring down at me like a crow in a tree. He was balanced on the railing above, clinging to the bars with his hands and bare feet. How he got up there so quickly, I had no idea. It was eight feet above the deck; he couldn't have jumped.

Could he?

"How did you get up there?" I asked. I looked for a ladder or rope but didn't see either. Then he let go of the bar, dropped to the deck without a sound, bounced on the steel floor, and went right back up, all in one movement. His body squeezed into a ball at the bottom, and sprang up as if he didn't weigh anything at all. As he neared the top, he reached for the railing and pulled himself the rest of the way up in one smooth movement, like a cat. It was absolutely remarkable to see.

"Ninjutsu," he said. "Mind and body are one."

Cool. He was a ninja! That meant that he was a warrior,

which meant that he could fight. Suddenly I was glad I hadn't brought a weapon on board. What if he thought I was an enemy and attacked me? He didn't look like a violent person. On the other hand, he didn't look like somebody who could jump eight feet in the air.

At least I knew now that he wasn't a ghost. He was trained in the secret art of ninjutsu, and that was why I had not been able to find him. But what on earth was he doing on this ship?

Chapter Three

∾

ONCE HE TOOK a look over the side and saw the sub, he seemed to lose interest in me. I didn't know why but I was pretty sure he was just waiting for me to leave so he could get back to whatever it was he had been doing before I came along. But what could he be doing all alone on an abandoned ship in the middle of the ocean?

I had no idea but I also had no reason to hang around, so I said goodbye respectfully, bowed my head—because he had bowed to me—climbed down the rope, jumped inside the sub, and started up the engine. What a strange old man was all I could think.

But as I put the sub in gear and started to pull away, I remembered that I hadn't seen a single thing to eat or drink on the ship, and I wondered how the old man was surviving. The thought that he might be hungry kept nagging at me, so after a couple of minutes I cut the engine and just let the sub drift. I had to sit down and think about it.

When you are alone on the sea, you always want to believe that somebody will come and help you if you need it. It is kind of an unwritten rule. The sea doesn't recognize differences between people. It doesn't care if you are rich or poor, young or old; it doesn't play favourites. You learn that pretty fast on the water. If you see someone in trouble, you go and help them, no questions asked. Someday it might be you.

And so, even though it might not be welcome, I decided to bring the old man something to eat and drink, and then I'd be on my way. Better to err on the side of helping someone out, I figured, no matter who he was. Maybe it would just irritate him if I climbed on board once more. I didn't know, but I knew I'd feel better if I left food and water behind.

So I returned to the side of the ship and moored the sub once more. I filled a jar with stew I had made the day before, and put it into the tool bag. Then I took a quick glance at my supplies, and added half a loaf of dried bread, two carrots, and a jug of water. That was a little more than I really wanted to leave, but I figured I'd better do it. Maybe the old man was starving. As strong as he obviously was, he *was* pretty skinny. I swung the bag over my shoulder, and climbed back up the rope.

Once again, there was no one on deck, so I walked around and waited. It didn't take long for him to show up. He appeared right behind me again, without a sound. One minute he wasn't there; the next, he was.

I turned and looked him in the eye. He was about two or three inches shorter than me. In some way he seemed a lot younger than he was. He was incredibly energetic; you could see it in his eyes. I had always heard that eyes are windows into the soul. If that were true then his soul was very young and bursting with energy.

"I brought you some stew," I said, "and a few other things to eat." I pulled the bag from my shoulder. In a flash the old man was on top of it. He opened it and looked inside. I wondered if he didn't trust me. He looked up at me, down at the food, and back up at me. He was frowning now, and the sadness was all over his face. I wondered how long it had been since he had eaten.

"This is for me?" he said.

I nodded. "Yes. If you want it."

He stood up and stared at the bag for a long time without really looking at it. His mind was somewhere else. I reached down, lifted the food and water out, swung the bag over my shoulder, and started to leave. When I was at the top of the rope, he made an odd sound, half between a cry and a laugh.

"Wait!" he cried. "Please wait."

I hesitated. I didn't really feel like it. I wanted to leave now. But he sounded so anxious that I shrugged and went back. He stuck out his hand and we shook. His hand dwarfed mine, and was as coarse as sandpaper.

"Can I show you something?" he said.

I sighed. "Okay."

So I followed him up a ladder to the bridge, and then up another ladder to the top of the bridge, where there was nothing but a few rusted air vents and a sealed bench that was probably once used for life jackets, but was now almost certainly empty. Everything had been stripped from this ship: the lights, the tools, the brass fittings. My guess was that they had stripped her before cutting her up for recycling, but that she had broken free in a storm before they had a chance to start, and they had never bothered to search for her. How the old man ended up on her was a mystery though.

He stood in front of the bench. It was an iron box about fifteen feet long, two and a half feet wide, and two and a half feet high. Like everything else on the ship, it was rusted so badly I doubted it would ever open again. I was wrong. The old man grabbed the lid and swung it open in one quick jerk, letting the lid fall back. I stared in awe. Inside was a garden! I saw at least a dozen tomato plants, heavy with ripe tomatoes; onions, or what looked like onions; garlic; and some leafy plants that looked like spinach. Everything was growing in a reddish-green soil that had bits of shell and seaweed in it. Once the lid was open, the sun poured into the bench and made the plants glow. What a transformation! The old man smiled from ear to ear.

"This is amazing," I said. I was really impressed.

Next, he led me down to the main deck, down a ladder to the lower, wrap-around deck, where lifeboats had once hung from ropes and pulleys. All of that was gone now. What remained were six benches, rusted so badly you would have thought they had been on the bottom of the sea for a hundred years. Once again the old man opened them. He must have filed and oiled their hinges. I couldn't believe what was inside.

The first two were filled with buckets of jellyfish. The buckets held water, and the jellyfish were alive. Inside the second two were buckets filled with chunks of fish. It might have been shark. I couldn't really tell, but the flesh was cut neatly into cubes and was floating in seawater. The first of the last two benches revealed a grill when the old man opened it. This was where he did his cooking. The last one was where he kept his tools. He had rope, hooks, knives, poles, and what looked like a sword in a cloth sheath.

I didn't know why he was showing me all of this but it was pretty interesting. Why would he trust me to see it?

"Would you like to stay and eat with me?" he asked.

Nothing I had seen looked very inviting, except for the vegetables. But I didn't want to insult him, so I said, "Yes, thank you."

Chapter Four

⁂

IT WAS AND WASN'T a satisfying meal. It didn't bother me to eat jellyfish because there were too many in the sea. They were the only things thriving when everything else was dying. But I wished the old man wasn't killing sharks. I was pretty sure it was shark. It was fishy and oily. The jellyfish was actually pretty good, grilled with garlic, onions, and tomatoes. You would have thought you were eating chips at a roadside diner. For drink we had water, which tasted like iron. He must have collected it in buckets when it rained.

While the old man cooked, I went down the rope for Hollie, put him in the tool bag, and carried him up on my back. He was excited. But we very narrowly avoided a terrible tragedy. Just as I reached the top of the rope, I saw the old man on the roof of the bridge. He had his sword in his hands in front of him. It was glistening in the sun as he sneaked up on Seaweed, who, unbelievably, didn't see him coming. "*Noooooooo!*" I screamed. Seaweed heard me, saw the old man, and jumped into the air. I shuddered to think that if I had been ten seconds slower, the old man would have served up my first mate for lunch. I could understand that his survival depended upon eating whatever was available, but I had to make it clear that Seaweed was part of my crew, not just some passing bird.

With Hollie it was a different story. The old man took one look at him and melted. They stared into each other's eyes, which is unusual for a dog to do with a stranger, and means that he feels a lot of trust. The old man patted him from head to tail. He rolled around with him on the deck, barked at him, and tried to play hide and seek, except that Hollie never had a chance. Like me, he never thought to look straight up whenever the old man disappeared, and he jumped just like I had when the old man suddenly reappeared.

When we sat down to eat, I saw a shadow of sadness creep into the old man's face again, just like a cloud in front of the sun. But once he put food into his mouth, his face changed again as joy spread across it, and that made me wonder if he had just been hungry. On the other hand, when I offered him some of my bread and stew, he shook his head and passed them back to me with a polite smile. I guess he wasn't that hungry. Or maybe he was only interested in eating food that he had prepared himself. Fair enough.

I wanted to learn his name, because you didn't really know someone if you didn't know his name. So I said, "I'm Alfred." Then I pointed to the crew. "That's Hollie, and that's Seaweed."

"Your crew?" He looked surprised.

"Yes."

He turned towards Seaweed, bowed respectfully, and said, "Alfred?"

"No. That's Seaweed."

Then he turned to Hollie, bowed again, and said, "Seaweed?"

"No. That's Hollie."

I didn't know which was stranger: that I had a dog and seagull crew, or that he was bowing to them. At least I felt confident now he wouldn't eat them.

After lunch the old man wanted to see how strong I was. I was glad. I thought he would be impressed with how well I could climb up the rope. The two exercises I always did on the sub were pull-ups and riding the stationary bike. I rode the bike every day because it was hooked up to the propeller shaft, and so, not only was it good exercise, but ten hours of pedalling generated about one hour of battery power. For pull-ups I fitted a bar inside the portal so that I could hang.

I could do fifteen pull-ups in a row now, and did three or four sets every day. It had taken me a couple of years to get that strong.

The old man wanted to see me do the rope. "Show me how you climb," he said, and made a gesture with his fist. He had a mix of gentleness and strength in his expressions that made me think he must have been a good teacher, because I found myself wanting to impress him. I couldn't help it.

So I climbed onto the rope and shinnied down as quickly as I could, landed on the hull, and shinnied back up. On the way up I heard the old man slapping his hands together. He wanted me to go faster, but I was going as fast as I could. It wasn't exactly easy. If you made a slight mistake, you would fall into the sea.

When I reached the top, I was out of breath. I wasn't used to climbing quite so fast. But the old man wanted me to do it again, faster. "Just a minute," I told him. I needed to catch my breath. But he wouldn't wait. He jumped from the deck, caught the rope on his way down, and slid down nearly as fast as you would go if you fell. His hands and feet were wrapped around the rope, and I couldn't understand why the rope didn't burn them. He reached the sub, let out a yell, and then scrambled back up the way a kid would climb the stairs with his hands and feet. He was *fast*. Watching him do it made me think that I could do it, too. I just needed to use his technique. I was starting to realize that I might actually learn something from this old man.

So I took a kind of awkward jump from the deck, trying to imitate him, and reached for the rope on the way down, which I very luckily caught but almost missed, and tried to slide down the way he had. But my hands and feet quickly started to overheat with the friction of the rope, and I had to stop a few times, otherwise I would have ended up with terrible blisters. It was fun though. Then, when I landed on the sub, I gave a yell. I looked up and saw the old man waving his fist at me, yelling at me to come back up.

So I tried to climb the same way. I grabbed the rope one hand at a time, but couldn't seem to grip it with my feet the way he had, the way a monkey climbs. I reached for it but my feet only pushed it away. It was a skill I just didn't have, and so my arms had to do all the work. It wasn't like shinnying, where you can rest by squeezing the rope against your body; this was all hands and feet. Halfway up, the muscles in my arms turned to jelly, and then they turned to lead. I made a desperate attempt to squeeze the rope against my body, but my hands wouldn't grip anymore. I lost my hold and went headfirst into the sea. It wasn't far, and didn't hurt much, but all I could hear when I raised my head out of the water was the old man laughing, like a kookaburra.

He jumped into the air, caught the rope, slid down to the sub, and was there to help me climb out of the water. I didn't need his help, and wondered if he was just showing off. But when we both stood on the hull, and he slapped my shoulder in a friendly way and said, "Good try," I realized he was actually trying to encourage me. Then he grabbed the rope and went back up just as fast as I had come down. As I watched him go, I thought: this is probably the strongest old man in the world.

I climbed the rope three more times, until my arms ached so badly I had to sit down, and could only watch as the old man did one-legged squats, one-arm push-ups, push-ups from a handstand, and jumps. He made it all look easy, but just watching him made me feel exhausted. It was hard to believe he was as old as he was, yet you could see it on his face and arms and legs, like a very old tree with smooth bark, with deep wrinkles where the branches stuck out.

He seemed pleased to have me around, but maybe he was just glad to have company. I knew I couldn't have impressed him much with my strength, yet he seemed keen to teach me anyway, and kept trying to coax me off the deck to join him in really hard exercises. What he didn't seem to understand was that I was completely wasted. There was no way I could do any more until I had rested. I didn't know how he had become so strong except that it must have taken him years and years of practice.

But why was he on this ship? And how was he keeping her afloat?

Well, that was the next thing he showed me.

Chapter Five

∽

"WHY ARE YOU HERE? Why are you on this ship?"

He looked me in the eye, and I saw something that took me back to when I was twelve, when I first saw the old oil tank that would eventually become my submarine. I had such a yearning for it, such an ache to go to sea in it I could hardly sleep. I couldn't think of anything else and would have done almost anything to have it. I was pretty sure I was seeing that kind of yearning in his eyes, as old as he was.

"Come," he said with an excited smile. "I will show you."

So I followed him.

There were three holds on the ship: fore, aft, and mid-ship.

There was a faint, musty, chemical odour coming from them, though they had probably been used to carry many things over the years: rock, coal, wood, grain, rice, fertilizer, anything really. Maybe they had carried guns and ammunition during the war, although I didn't know if the ship was really that old.

At the aft hold, the old man turned to me and smiled. I could tell he loved secrets. He reached down, unlocked a hatch with a lever, and lifted it up. It looked very heavy but he swung it open with ease. I didn't know why I hadn't seen the lever before; it was right in front of me. He gestured for me to look. So I bent down and peered inside. At first, it was too dark to see, so I clicked on my flashlight. What a surprise! The hold was nearly filled with plastic. There were plastic bottles, sheets, buckets, toys, benches, chairs, roofing, flooring, animals, and pieces impossible to identify because they had been in the water too long. All of it was plastic. But . . . where had it come from? I was confused.

Then he showed me the other holds, and they were the same. I stood in awe. "Where has it come from?" I asked.

He gestured with his arms opened wide. "The sea."

"But how? Did you pull it out of the water, *piece by piece*?"

He nodded his head, and I knew it was true. Wow! Suddenly my respect for him grew a hundred times. He was doing exactly what I wanted to do.

Then he showed me something else. At the back wall of the fore-hold was a shaft that stretched from the floor to the ceiling, up through the floor above, and onto the deck where it supported a derrick and boom that were once used to load and unload cargo. There were much larger doors in the holds, of course, that could swing up and open, like barn doors, for loading cargo, but they were shut and sealed tight to keep the rain and waves out. The boom and pulleys were no longer here, but the shaft was, although it was another one of those parts of the ship that blended into the background so well you didn't really see it. It didn't help that everything was dark inside the hold too. The old man gestured for me to follow him inside. So I did.

It was a strange feeling to jump into the plastic. Most of it was soft against my skin because it had been in the sea for so long, but some was sharp edged, and I had to be careful not to get cut. Moving through it was a little like swimming. The old man led me straight to the shaft, where, at the bottom, there was a drain in the floor. It was a challenge to swim down through the plastic to get there, harder still to breathe, and too dark to see anything without my flashlight. As I stared at the drain, I got a spooky feeling because it looked as though it led to somewhere that was not on the ship, as impossible as that was. When you stood on the floor of the hold, with a mountain of plastic above you, you really felt you were on the bottom floor of the ship, but you weren't actually. Beneath the hold was a subfloor, and the drain went down there.

The old man lifted the grate, pushed it up through the

plastic, and squeezed it against the shaft. Then he wormed his way down into the drain, gesturing with his arm for me to follow. I didn't like that at all but I squeezed through the drain and lowered myself into about two feet of water. It was completely black but with the flashlight I could see the silhouette of the old man. He grabbed my elbow a few times to direct me where to go. I didn't like the feeling of standing in water where I couldn't see anything. What if there were sea snakes in here?

The old man pulled me to one side of the shaft. Then he lifted up a metal plate, and I saw a dim light. Now I could see his face. It felt as though we were inside a mine, deep underground. He gestured for me to stick my head inside the shaft, where the light was coming from, so I peered inside and looked up. The shaft went straight up to where it was shiny and bright at the top. There was a wire pulley system inside, and buckets, seven or eight of them, which were attached to the wires. The old man squeezed his arm in next to my face, grabbed hold of the wire, and pulled it down. I saw the buckets move. He kept pulling until a bucket came all the way down and splashed into the water. It filled about halfway as it went around the bottom and began its journey up. Amazing! The old man had created his own manual pumping machine. This was how he was emptying the water from the ship.

But the real lifting he did from the top, on the derrick. When we climbed out of the hold, he led me up, removed a plate from the shaft where it was exposed outside, and I saw where the real work was done, where you could pull on the wire with both hands, and put your body into it. He gestured for me to try it, and so I did. I pulled down on the wire and watched as bucket after bucket came up slowly inside the shaft, tilted, and spilled water onto the deck. At first it seemed easy. But after just ten buckets or so, my arms began to burn again, my hands cramped up, and I had to stop. The old man took my place and pulled on the wire twice as fast. The buckets came flying up and spilled water like rain. Once again it might have looked as though he was showing off, but he wasn't. He was instructing me.

The longer I watched him, the more I realized he really just wanted to teach somebody. Okay, I thought: I am happy to learn. So I smiled and nodded my head. He closed the shaft, took a step back, and slapped his chest. Then, finally, he told me his name.

"I am Sensei."

Chapter Six

✍

SENSEI HAD ONE more secret to share, and it was a good one. He showed me in the afternoon, when the wind began to gust from the west. At the base of the two remaining derricks, in the fore and aft, were two more rusted benches, which, when opened, revealed what looked like large folded tarps. On the fore-derrick Sensei pulled on a wire I hadn't paid any attention to before, and the tarp rose out of the bench and began to climb the derrick just like handkerchiefs pulled out of a magician's pocket. It was a sail! It was a patchwork sail sewn together from about twenty pieces of canvas, nylon, and rugged cotton. He raised a similar one in the stern. They must have taken forever to sew. The sails caught the wind, and I felt a gentle tug beneath my feet as the ship came round. Astonished, I followed Sensei onto the bridge and into the pilothouse where he took hold of the wheel. Like an old whale that had all but forgotten how to swim, the battered ship turned sluggishly into the wind and began to sail. She couldn't have been doing more than four knots, but she was moving, and Sensei was steering her.

"This is amazing!" I shouted. Sensei beamed with pride.

Rightly so. She was the furthest thing from a streamlined vessel, yet there was a sense of dignity about her, as if under the power of the wind she had more right to be on the water than if she were powered by engines.

I wondered if he had once been an engineer, because he was so skilled at mechanical things. On the other hand, he seemed to have a special kind of relationship with everything he touched. It took me a while to understand that. I followed him around as he tended his garden like a monk on a mountaintop, pumped water out of the hull like a field worker, did exercises like a circus acrobat, and stood at the helm of his ship like an ancient mariner. He did everything with grace and care such as I had never seen anyone show for anything before. Every action was measured and thought-out and enjoyed as if he were living in a more orderly kind of universe than the one I knew. And yet, in spite of all of that, he carried sadness around with him like a ball and chain, and it would pull him down whenever he wasn't busy or focused on something. What, I wondered, was that about? But I didn't want to ask, and he didn't offer to say.

The one thing he didn't do much was talk. With the exception of telling me his name, and a few short sentences here and there, he went about his tasks with monk-like silence. The strange result was that, after a few days in his company, I started to talk as if I had nothing better to do than flap my lips. I simply couldn't seem to shut up. I wasn't sure why I was doing it, except that maybe I felt uncomfortable with his silence. Weren't people supposed to talk when they were doing things together?

That made me wonder about how much I talked on the sub to the crew. I wasn't sure. In any case, I decided to spend a couple of weeks on the ship, from early morning till sunset each day, following Sensei around and learning from him. And for most of the first few days, I talked non-stop, until I couldn't stand the sound of my voice anymore. It usually sounded something like this:

"I'm from Newfoundland. That's in Canada. Where are you from? How old are you? Do you mind me asking? Today is my birthday, actually. I'm seventeen today. I first went to sea when I was fourteen. Hollie and Seaweed are my crew. They've been with me pretty much from the beginning. I rescued Hollie from a drifting dory. Somebody threw him off a wharf with a rope tied around his neck, but he landed in a dory. Isn't that terrible? Seaweed just joined me one day. I don't think he's a normal seagull actually; he seems to think he's an eagle or something. He's really tough, though, but kind of moody. Do you get moody? I get moody. Where do you get the soil for your garden? Do you compost? It looks like you're composting seaweed and shells. That's pretty good for a garden, I bet. Your garden is awesome. Where did you learn to garden anyway? I'm glad you're showing me how to do things, but I don't see how I can keep a garden on the sub. There isn't enough room, and not enough sunlight. How old are you anyway? Can you tell me that at least . . . ?"

He raised his head and gazed at me. "One hundred years."

"Really? Wow."

I didn't get a lot of answers, but that one shut me up for a while.

The first thing Sensei did every morning was sit on top of the bridge, face the sun, and meditate. Once we were out of bed, Hollie and I would join him, and do that for about an hour. Sensei sat with his eyes closed. I would start like that but couldn't stay that way for long. In the first place, Hollie would demand my attention the moment my eyes were shut. And while Sensei was perfectly able to ignore his new friend, even if he was pawed by him, I'd have to open my eyes and respond. And then I'd stare at the sea. I couldn't help it. I was trained to keep watch for ships and things, and since I couldn't hear the radar beep from the sub, I felt kind of blind.

Luckily we were travelling in currents that didn't cross shipping lanes. So far I hadn't seen a single vessel, although one could have passed when we weren't watching. I wondered how Sensei spotted them when he wasn't watching. I mean, he had to know it was important. Other ships would have radar, of course, and they'd see Sensei's ship coming from miles away, but they'd surely expect him to manoeuvre politely out of the way, which he couldn't do very well when the sails were down. He could turn the rudder with the wheel, and the ship might eventually respond, but it was the slowest thing in the world, even under sail.

The second thing Sensei did each morning was pump water. Keeping the water to a safe level was almost a full-time job for one person. If it pooled too much it could create a wave inside when the ship was tossing and pitching, causing her to lean too far to one side. If she got hit by a large wave when she was leaning like that, she'd capsize.

We took turns pulling on the wire, although he pulled twice as fast and for about three times as long as I did. I didn't know why the wire didn't hurt his hands. It blistered mine terribly because the wire was rusty and wet. I showed him my hands on the third day because the blisters had broken and I was a little concerned about getting rust in my blood and needing a tetanus shot, which I couldn't get anywhere around here.

I wondered what he did when he got sick. Did he get sick? I asked him but all he did was take one look at my hands and then slap them together really hard, which made them sting. Then he gestured for me to keep slapping them, which I did, until the stinging went away and was replaced by a hot throbbing in my hands, which was better. Then I could pull on the wire again. Talk about tough medicine.

The third thing Sensei did was a series of exercises. By then I was pretty hungry, but Sensei didn't touch a bite of food or water for the first two hours of the day.

We did single leg squats first, which were hard to do when you weren't used to them, and almost impossible to do with good balance. Sensei did them with perfect balance. He tucked one leg behind the other and went down and up as smoothly as an engine piston in slow motion. He was absolutely tireless. After just ten or so, my leg was burning, and I couldn't wait to change legs, and then change back. I did three or four sets. Sensei did ten, with twenty-five reps in each one.

Then we did calf raises by standing on the edge of a bench with the toes of one foot gripping the metal. Down and up we went like roosters strutting up and down on a fence. I started to laugh, and had to hold onto the wall to keep from falling. Sensei didn't hold onto anything; his balance was perfect.

Next we did one-arm push-ups, which I found hardest of all, but managed to do about three, without going all the way down. Sensei did so many I lost count. Then we did pull-ups, the one exercise in which I felt I had something to show for myself. To my fifteen repetitions Sensei did a hundred, and three sets of them, which meant *three hundred pull-ups* every day! His body was light, and he did them quickly. No wonder he was so strong.

For the rest of the day, Sensei tended his garden, kept his eyes on the sea, and occasionally raised the sails. But sailing was not his priority. As far as I could tell, he raised the sails solely for the purpose of correcting his course, in order to stay in the circular current. He was more interested in moving at the speed of the water than the speed of the wind. The reason for this was his purpose for being on the sea in the first place—cleaning up the plastic.

Sensei could detect plastic beneath the surface of the waves almost like a French pig could sniff out a truffle. I saw that on TV once. Perhaps it was the way the water pooled above an object and created a tiny wake, I wasn't sure, but he could see things I couldn't. Sometimes I would, and sometimes I wouldn't.

From a bench on the stern he lifted out a fishing net and ropes. Whenever he spied something, we'd lower the net, grab the object, and haul it up. Sometimes it was just a single thing, like a plastic table, and sometimes it was a patch of things that looked as though an ocean liner had dumped its garbage. We'd find plastic plates, forks, knives and spoons, plastic lawn chairs, umbrellas, bottles of shampoo, bags, and on and on.

But we'd also find fishing nets. Either they had been cut loose by fishermen after they had become entangled, or had been simply swept off boats and wharfs in stormy weather.

The result was always the same—rotting sea creatures that had been unable to free themselves.

We found a shocking number of seabirds, turtles, dolphins, fish, and sharks. I now realized Sensei didn't kill sharks. He would examine a rotting corpse, cut it open with his sword, smell it, taste it, and then decide if the meat was edible. He was the ultimate scavenger. He didn't waste an ounce of anything.

∽

When it was finally time to eat, I'd be absolutely starving. I'd follow Sensei to the garden, where we'd choose tomatoes, onions, greens and garlic, and carry them down to the grill. Then we'd grab some driftwood from where he had stashed it in one of the holds, break apart a log, snap off a few branches, and carry it up to the deck.

Next, he would have me pull some jellyfish from one of the buckets. I'd cup the heads in my hands without touching the tentacles, and lift them out, but sometimes they'd slip out of my hands and fall onto the deck. So I'd have to grab them, tentacles and all, and pick them up. It would sting, but you develop a kind of immunity if you get stung a lot, which I did.

When the fire was glowing, Sensei would lay chunks of shark and vegetables on the grill, and gesture for me to lay the jellyfish down, which I would, watching the tentacles curl like elastic bands at first, and then relax and stretch out like spaghetti.

As I watched the jellyfish cook, I drifted away in my mind. I had reached a point in my life where I could no longer eat animals. I wasn't one hundred percent certain, but I was pretty sure. When I had been in the Southern Ocean, just a couple of months earlier, I had witnessed a blue whale being killed right in front of me. Somehow, looking into her eye as she was dying, I realized I could never kill another creature that could look me back in the eye and know what I was doing. I wasn't sure about fish. I needed more time to think about it. I wouldn't kill sharks though, because their numbers were falling drastically in the sea, and I wouldn't kill any species that was threatened.

But jellyfish were taking over the sea. So I didn't mind eating them. All the same, watching a living creature shrivel up and die bothered me.

It never bothered Sensei. He would grin triumphantly whenever the jellyfish would spit and sizzle in the flames.

Chapter Seven

⋘

FOR SOME REASON Sensei wouldn't come inside the sub. He'd stand on the hull, but not step inside. I couldn't figure out why. He wasn't afraid; I knew that. He wasn't afraid of anything, as far as I could tell.

"You should come inside and see my sub. It's pretty cool. We finished it three years ago. It took us two and a half years to build. Ziegfried built it actually; I just helped him. I wonder what you'd think of Ziegfried. He's pretty much a giant. You'd be amazed. He's probably the strongest man in New-foundland."

I stared at Sensei to see if he would react to that. I thought maybe he was grinning a little, but I wasn't sure.

"He can pick up the front end of a truck all by himself."

He raised his eyebrows. He was impressed.

"I wonder who would win if you were in a fight. That would be interesting. He's not a skilled fighter like you probably are but I think he'd win. You wouldn't be able to hit him hard enough to hurt him, I think, and then, once he grabbed hold of you, you'd never get away. He also happens to be a genius, so you probably wouldn't stand a chance. No offence."

Sensei looked over at me, smiled, and dropped his head.

"Ziegfried's married to Sheba now. Sheba is the most remarkable woman in the world. She's an oracle. She can read your future in cards, and interpret dreams. She loves everybody and everything. You would love her too; you wouldn't be able to help it. It's like a spell she puts on you. She's also a great gardener. She would be very impressed with your garden. I wish she could see it."

Sensei raised his head again and smiled. He was pleased.

"Sheba grows flowers, vegetables, and mushrooms in her kitchen. She lives in a house on a tiny island where it's always foggy. Ziegfried and Sheba are sort of like parents to me. My mother died when I was born, and my father lives in Montreal, but he left when I was born. I went to visit him last year for the first time and discovered that I have a little sister, too, but I haven't stayed in touch with them as much as I'd like to. It's hard when you're at sea."

Sensei nodded. Sadness was hovering around him now

like a gloomy day. It was in his voice. "To lose family is very difficult."

"That's true. But I'm going to visit them as soon as I return to Canada. I'm sort of on my way home now, but I wanted to come to Japan to meet the people who kill whales because I need to understand why humans are destroying the planet. I think that if I can meet the people who kill whales, the most gentle and intelligent creatures on the planet, I might understand the bigger problem better. Maybe I can't change their minds, but at least I can learn why they don't care."

I stopped talking and looked over. He was nodding in agreement. It was nearly impossible to get him to say more than a few words at a time but at least he was listening.

I noticed he was suddenly holding two poles in his hands. Where did *they* come from? They weren't there two seconds ago. They looked like wooden swords. He turned and threw one into the air towards me. I reached for it but missed. It struck me on the side of the head and fell onto the deck with a rattle. It didn't hurt much because it was so light. I stared at it for a moment before picking it up. I had a feeling that the second I touched it, I was in trouble. I *could* just leave it there, and pretend I wasn't interested . . . like a chicken, or I could grab it and defend myself.

I picked it up. It was light in my hands, like bamboo, and felt good. He stood and faced me. He was smiling, but it was a serious kind of smile. "When you want to stop," he said, "you just say . . . '*give up*'."

Give up? Was he serious? I hated those words. I hated them more than anything. Giving up was the one thing I never did. If I were going to give up, I might just as well have stayed home and worked on my grandfather's boat. Sensei was in for a surprise if he thought I was ever going to give up.

The second I raised my wooden sword, his sword swung through the air with a flash of colour and tapped my ear. It stung just like a bee. "*Ouch!*" I tried to duck, but he struck me again. Oh boy.

"Give up?" he said.

"No!"

As hopeless at it might have seemed, the feeling of the sword in my hand gave me such a sense of power that I thought maybe, just maybe, I might surprise him. I wouldn't rush in and foolishly expect to strike him right away, knowing what a superior fighter he probably was. Instead, I would play the innocent, and lure him into a trap. I would pretend I couldn't handle the stick as well as I actually could, and wait for him to let down his guard. I had to hit him only once, just once, for him to feel my sting. And that gave me more determination than I think I've ever felt in all of my life.

And so began the stick fight on the ship, a crazy kind of fight that started out as a simple lesson but became for me a very painful one.

Sensei's method of teaching fighting was brutally simple: I'm going to keep hitting you until you learn how to defend yourself. If you hurt too much, you just have to say, "give up."

But defending yourself against someone who can jump eight feet in the air, who has lightning reflexes, and years of training, is hardly easy. For the first hour or so I received so many hits with the stick that my body ached all over. My ears were inflamed and burning. The bones of my skull were sore. My elbows hurt, my back stung as if I had been whipped, my feet were so sore they were almost numb, my upper lip was swollen, and I think my front teeth were a little loose. But painful as it was, it never crossed my mind to quit, and I think that surprised Sensei, and maybe even shocked him a little. He kept saying, "give up?" And I would answer, "*No!* I don't give up!"

Even as he was inflicting pain on me, I stayed on my feet and ran around the ship. He was laughing a lot of the time, seeming to have fun in a serious sort of way. He'd disappear, and reappear, most often right behind me. But I learned to look for that, and guess when he might show up. If the sticks had been real swords, I would have been dead in the first ten seconds. I knew that. And I did wonder if he realized just how much pain he was inflicting. He must have known. Still, neither of us could give up. I was too fired up, and he seemed to be just as locked into having to hear me say "give up" as I was in refusing to ever say it.

And then, in one glorious moment, I discovered his weakness. Yes, he did have a weakness, though he had hidden it from me all this time. It involved his aerobic capacity. Sensei was like dynamite for quick bursts of energy. He could jump, run, swing, stab, and exercise in so many ways for anywhere from ten seconds to about two minutes. But then he needed to stop and catch his breath. Up to two minutes he could do almost anything. But after that point he would lose his breath. Because his body simply wasn't getting enough oxygen, he'd have to stop and let his lungs breathe in and fill up, and give his muscles a chance to regain their strength before he could continue. And once he was in that state of needing oxygen, he was vulnerable.

This was the difference between us. Except for the pull-ups I did every day, my main exercise was riding the stationary bike on the sub, which I did for hours at a time, so my lung capacity was really strong. When I was on land I could walk for days before I got tired. Sensei's exercises were all bursts of energy that lasted for only a minute at a time, except for when he ran around the ship. But I never saw him run for more than a few minutes at a time, and that was why he didn't have great aerobic capacity. It might also have been because he was a hundred years old.

Once I understood this difference between us, I began to use it to my advantage. At one point, I watched Sensei stop chasing me, bend over, and catch his breath. As soon as I saw that, I turned around and swung my stick at him, but he picked himself up, blocked my swing, and hit me. So I ran again.

Before long, he stopped again, and did the same thing. That's when I realized I just needed to wear him out. And so, instead of running fast, as I was doing, I slowed down my pace a little so that I could keep it up longer. I ran around and around the deck, and up on the bridge, and back down, with Sensei following me, hitting me on the side of the head, or at the elbow, or on my feet, but each time it was weaker now, and he was getting slower. I was wearing him out!

The first time I struck Sensei with the stick I could hardly believe it, and neither could he. Unlike him, I swung with all my might. I hadn't yet learned to swing more gently and efficiently, with control. I just swung wildly, expecting as always to strike at air. But the stick hit Sensei on the arm just below the shoulder, with a cracking sound, as if I had hit the side of the ship. It was a hard strike, and though it bounced off his muscles like a sponge ball, I knew that he felt it. It must have stung.

But if it did, he didn't show it. Instead, he immediately rushed in and struck me just as hard. He hit me on the leg, and it really burned. I didn't care; I had inflicted pain on my attacker. I felt like a king—bruised and beaten-up, but a king no less.

Chapter Eight

 birds

I WAS SLEEPING. I had left the hatch open to let fresh air in. Sleeping with the hatch open was almost like sleeping outside, except that you didn't get wet if it rained, and the wind could seep in softly, and was warm on your skin.

Hollie was on his blanket on one side of the observation window, and Seaweed was on the other. I had fallen asleep with the sound of Hollie snoring, which I could hear only when the sea was calm. I remember feeling in my sleep that there was someone in the sub, but I didn't pay it much mind. Many sailors speak of ghosts that visit their vessels while they sleep, or while they are below deck in storms. It was a feeling I often had, too, so much in fact that I had learned to stop worrying about it.

But in the middle of the night, I woke to the most horrible sound. There was a banging on the outside of the hull, and a frightening, hideous crying, as if an animal were being attacked and killed by another animal. It was awful. Had some creature grabbed another and taken it to the sub to dismember it? This is what ran through my mind even as I knew there couldn't be any kind of animal in the middle of the Pacific Ocean. There might be a bird, such as a long-distance seabird, although I didn't think it would sound like that even if it were being killed. And what would be killing it?

As the poor creature wailed pitifully for its life, I meant to jump to my feet and rescue it. But the moment I tried to rise from my bed, I felt something tighten around my hands and feet and bind them. I raised my head. I had been tied to my bed!

"Sensei?" I yelled. I knew it had to be him. "Sensei?"

There was no answer. The noise outside the hull had stopped. I tried with all my might to pull my hands and feet free, but it was impossible. Struggling only made the knots tighter. I was trapped. I was powerless. What a horrible feeling. How could I have let this happen?

"Sensei?"

I waited and waited but he never came. It was the middle of the night, when my fears were always strongest. What if Sensei never came back? What if he was truly crazy, and this was his way of punishing me for having struck him with the stick? These were the thoughts that raced through my head as I failed to free myself.

"Sensei?"

For what felt like hours, I fought against my confinement. I pulled and twisted and tugged until my whole body was sore and sweating. It was only when I stopped fighting it, and calmed down, that I was able to think it through and come up with a plan to rescue myself.

"Hollie," I said quietly. He had been sitting next to my bed the whole time, waiting for me to get up. "Bring me a knife. Bring me a knife, Hollie. Go get me a knife."

Eager to please, and used to bringing tools to Ziegfried and me, Hollie went to the stove, where the cooking utensils were stuck by magnets to the wall. He came back with a wooden stirring spoon.

"Good dog, Hollie. You are so smart. Now, go get me another one. Go get me a knife, Hollie. A *knife*."

It took three tries before he brought me a knife. He dropped it on the floor beside the bed.

"Up here, Hollie. Bring the knife up here."

He barked. He liked playing this game. He picked up the knife, jumped onto the bed, and dropped it onto my belly.

"You are so smart, Hollie. Good dog. What a good dog you are."

By twisting and raising my trunk I was able to slide the knife down to my left hand. Once I gripped it, I turned it upside down, and then began to slowly cut the plastic twine around my wrist. It was tricky to do without cutting myself, and it took a long time, but I cut my left hand free. Once one hand was free, I was free. I sat up on the edge of my bed and patted Hollie's fur.

"What a wonderful dog you are. What a wonderful friend. What do you think, Hollie? Should we leave now? Should we get away from this crazy old man? Or should we wait until tomorrow to decide?"

Hollie stared up at me and wagged his tail. He liked Sensei. They had become good friends. Hollie didn't have many friends.

"Okay. I think maybe he's crazy, but if you want to wait, we'll wait."

I climbed the portal, sealed the hatch from the inside, and put a bar in the wheel to lock it. Then I climbed back into my bed. It took a long time to get back to sleep. I knew I had to think about what had just happened but was too tired to make any sense of it now. My gut feeling was to leave, that this was all going too far. And yet another voice inside me made me wonder if there was a greater purpose in it. Was I learning something, or was I just being abused by a crazy old man? In the middle of the night, I really didn't know the answer to that question.

∽

In the morning everything looked different to me. I found Sensei in the middle of his meditation on top of the bridge, sitting like a monk under the morning sun. He didn't look at all like a crazy man now; he looked like a wise old sage. Just the sight of him filled me with respect. He was, after all, a hundred years old. *I* was the boy. Looking at him now, I realized his late-night prank was most definitely a lesson for me, a lesson in vigilance and stealth. An important lesson, too: don't leave yourself so foolishly vulnerable to attack. If Sensei could sneak in and tie me up so easily, what was I doing to prevent pirates from doing the same? Nothing.

As I sat down across from him he leaned forward slightly in a bow to welcome me. I bowed back. He was wearing a friendly smile. I couldn't quite bring myself to smile, and neither of us mentioned what had happened.

I had to get even though, not because I wanted to, but because I knew that he expected me to, even if he didn't say so in words. I just knew it. He was the teacher; I was the student. As kind and gentle as he was when we were not fighting, he was ruthless and disciplined when we were. He would expect retaliation, and in that way I would show that I had learned the lesson. But sneaking up on Sensei was easier said than done.

In the first place, I didn't know where he slept. He never showed me. But the very next night when it was late, I climbed out of the sub and shinnied up the rope as silently as I could. In my pack I carried a small can of grease. On the deck near the stern, where Sensei would often sprint in the morning, bounce off the railing, and jump high into the air,

I spread a thin layer of grease—not enough to be visible, but enough to turn the area into a skating rink. In truth, I never really thought it through; I just pictured Sensei sliding on the grease and flying into the railing. He would catch himself because he was too skilled not to, and wouldn't get hurt. But he might have a scare, just a tiny one, and then we would be even. It wasn't brilliant, but it was all I could think of. It never crossed my mind that anything worse might happen.

The next morning, I joined him for meditation. Afterwards, we did our exercises, pumped water, and ate breakfast. Then we pulled garbage from the sea. But all I could think of was when he would run down the passageway, slide on the grease, and slam into the railing. I would stand back and smile. I chuckled about it every time I thought of it.

As Murphy's Law would have it, Sensei didn't take his normal morning sprints, and kept avoiding that area as if he knew what I had done. Did he? I followed him around more closely than usual, and had to remind myself to avoid the slippery spot. I even wondered if he were trying to lead me onto it a few times. I couldn't help feeling impatient waiting for him to run down the deck and fall. But just when I had all but given up, he slapped me on the shoulder, clicked his tongue, and took off at lightning speed down the deck, right onto the grease. With wide eyes I watched him go. He hit the slippery patch, started to slide, lost his balance, hit the rail, and went right over the side of the ship.

I stood still, stunned. I never heard him hit the water, but that was not surprising because it was a long way down. I just stood there and stared for a while, half expecting him to poke his head up and laugh. But he never did. Suddenly it occurred to me that I had never actually seen Sensei swim. My mind raced as I tried to remember if I had ever seen him in the water. I didn't think so. I had seen him climb down the rope, and he had certainly climbed onto the sub, but had I ever actually seen him in the water? No. Did I know then that he could swim? No, I didn't. Therefore I had to assume that he couldn't. Many sailors and fishermen couldn't swim. Good Heavens.

I rushed to the railing, slipping and almost falling on the grease myself, and looked over the side. Luckily the ship wasn't sailing, so I didn't have to worry about him being left behind in its wake. But where was he? I scanned the water carefully, looking for his little head to come up, but it never did. Since muscle was heavier than fat, and a muscular person can't swim as easily as a flabby person, because they don't have as much buoyancy, and as Sensei didn't have any fat at all, maybe his body went straight to the bottom. The thought that I had just killed him by knocking him overboard horrified me. I jumped onto the rail, scanned the water below to make sure I wasn't jumping right on top of his head, and went over the side.

The jump pulled me under about ten feet before I could swim back up and search for him. I scanned the surface but he wasn't there, so I stuck my head under and began to look for him there.

I couldn't find him. I began to panic. How could I have been so stupid? What a ridiculous thing to do. Why hadn't I turned the other cheek? Why hadn't I trusted my own judgment? Please, please let me find him, I said over and over in my head. Don't let me kill this man.

For several minutes I searched as hard as I could. I swam down about thirty feet, turning in all directions frantically. If he had drowned, I would surely be able to find his body. He wouldn't sink so fast, would he? I really didn't know.

But I couldn't give up, so I resurfaced, took a deeper breath, and went down as deep as I could, about a hundred feet, and searched desperately. But it was darker there, and very hard to see, and it just felt futile. If Sensei *had* drowned, his body was probably several hundred feet down already, and falling. How horrible. What had I done?

I rose to the surface gasping for air. I was very upset. I had played a really stupid prank on an old man and had killed him. It couldn't be. It just couldn't.

Well . . . it wasn't. As soon as I raised my head out of the water and filled my lungs with air, I looked up and saw Sensei on the deck, staring down at me with a grin on his face.

"Give up?" he said.

Chapter Nine

∽

AFTER TWO WEEKS my body was more bruised and sore than it had ever been in all of my life. I had cuts on my hands and feet, cuts on my elbows and knees, bumps on my head, bruises on my face and back, and blisters on my fingers and toes. I was more beaten up than if I had been beaten up.

And yet I had become stronger and tougher. That felt good. When Sensei struck me with the stick, it still hurt, but not as much as it had at first. I could climb like never before, and was even starting to use my feet. Just two weeks of one-legged squats had almost doubled the height I could jump. I liked these changes very much. As beaten up as I was, I was hungry for more.

Even more surprising, I felt more sharply aware of the things around me: the sounds, shapes, and smells. Things that had blended into the background before now seemed more obvious. I felt more aware of the wind, how it shaped itself into little curls when it brushed up against me, and I could smell the tomatoes on the breeze from a farther distance. I even thought I could taste the sun and soil in their flesh. Where all this awareness was coming from I couldn't say exactly except that it had something to do with the extremes of physical challenges, and sitting quiet under the sun. There was something life-changing about struggling very hard physically. Meditation brought life-changes too, no doubt, but it was the exercise that affected me most. You wouldn't want always to seek it, I thought, but when it was in and around you, it brought a wonderfully heightened awareness with it.

I thought about all of this as I sat across from Sensei on top of the bridge under the early morning sun. I knew I wasn't supposed to think about anything when we were meditating. Meditating was all about getting away from your thoughts, your self, he had told me. "Don't think. Meditate." But I couldn't help it. I wasn't a tremendously good meditator. When we meditated, I mostly just pretended I was meditating. I couldn't help wondering if his need to escape his thoughts came from a need to avoid the sadness that haunted him.

Afterwards, when we did our exercises, I watched to see if he was noticing my growing strength. If he was, he didn't say so. He seemed impossible to impress, and that was an attitude that just made me work harder.

When it was time to eat, I was always starving. My appetite had doubled, and I probably would have eaten anything he put in front of me now: sea worms, slugs, bottom feeders . . . anything. I began to savour the taste of jellyfish. I was beginning to understand him better. When we tended the garden in the late morning, I held a ripe tomato in my hands and thought how perfect it was, and how beautiful. And my respect for the wisdom of the old man who had created this garden grew immensely.

But a little later that afternoon, we were back at fighting with the sticks, and the cuts on my elbows were starting to bleed, and the bumps on my head were hot, and my ears were ringing.

"Give up?" Sensei said. He never gave up saying it.

"No. I *don't* give up."

I took a peek over the edge of the ship, because sometimes I thought I might just jump over and swim to the sub for a rest. I would never do it, of course, even though the temptation was always there, to escape from a fight that I was always losing.

And yet I was also striking him more, and hitting harder, and leaving welts, which only made him more determined to punish me. It was a battle that I couldn't win, and yet couldn't quit.

But I never had to. Fate had something else in store for both of us.

∞

We had reached a moment when we were both taking a breather. I had managed to overwhelm Sensei's aerobic capacity once again, but it had taken me longer to do it, and so instead of rushing in and striking him, I had to bend over and catch my own breath. There was a lull in our combat then, and I even wondered if maybe he had had enough, too. Oddly, when I raised my head to look at him, I noticed a strange line on the horizon behind him. The horizon wasn't as still as before. I mean, it was level, but it wasn't as calm. Something had changed. That was odd. I wondered if things just looked different because I had been hit so many times.

I didn't think so. Sensei raised his stick. He intended to continue. So I raised mine, but I couldn't take my eyes away from the horizon. Sensei took advantage of my trance, reached over, and struck my ear. Oh, how it stung! "No!" I said. "Wait! Wait a second! Look!" I pointed out to sea. But Sensei would never fall for what he believed was a simple trick. Instead, he swung his stick and struck my foot. "Ouch! Stop! Stop for a second, will you? *Look!*" I pointed to the horizon. Sensei saw the true alarm on my face, stepped back, and took a very quick glance. Then we both just stood and stared.

The horizon was vibrating now. I couldn't figure it out. It was vibrating, and . . . it was growing! Oh my Lord, suddenly I knew what it was! It was a gigantic wave!

"*Tsunami!* Sensei! It's a *tsunami*! Hurry! We've got to get inside the sub! *Come!*" I gestured with my arm frantically. "We have to go . . . *now!*" But he shook his head. He shouted something in Japanese, and gestured for me to follow him into the stairwell that led to the holds.

"*No!* That's crazy! Come with me! The sub is our only chance!"

But he wouldn't. I grabbed Hollie and ran to the railing. "Sensei, please! Come with us!"

But he just shook his head and gestured for me to follow him. That was suicide. The wave was going to hit the ship on the starboard side. Judging from the distance, I was guessing it was a hundred feet high. There was no way any ship could survive such a wave striking on its side, and there was no time to turn the bow. She was going to capsize. Our only hope was to climb inside the sub and dive. I didn't even know if we had enough time to do that, but if we did, we'd survive. We'd be thrown around, but we'd survive. Staying on the ship was death.

But Sensei wouldn't come. So I held Hollie tightly and jumped over the side. The fall knocked him out of my arms, and when I came up, he was swimming in a circle ten feet away. He swam towards me, and I grabbed him and swam to the sub. We could hear the wave above us now, roaring like an avalanche. As I climbed onto the hull, the wave blocked out the sun. In a panic I jumped inside, dropped Hollie onto the floor, rushed back up the portal, and sealed the hatch. The sub began to rise, as the wave picked us up. I grabbed

Hollie once more and dived for my cot, squashing him beneath me. I held onto both sides of the bed with all my might as the sub went up and up and up. It seemed endless. Then we rolled upside down. Still I held onto the cot with Hollie beneath me.

On the crest of the wave we rolled once again until we were almost upright. But the ship was in our path. I knew that. And I knew that the wave would throw us against it, so I braced myself for the collision. When it came, it knocked me free of my grip, and Hollie and I were thrown around inside, banging off the walls and tumbling around and around as the sub rolled over the ship, bounced off, and rolled over it again. I feared the worst. If I saw water spilling inside, I would reach for Hollie, climb the portal, spin the hatch, and pull him out. There was no chance to take the dinghy, only the lifebuoy. Without the dinghy we wouldn't survive at sea for long.

But after we rolled over the ship the second time, the sub was thrown into the trough of the wave. It spun around and around in a whirlpool. I pulled myself over to the control panel and hit the dive switch. The sub was tossing and pitching like crazy, but once it righted itself it began to suck water into the ballast tanks and we started to submerge. Outside the hull there was a horrible sound—the twisting, bending, and tearing of metal as the sea ripped the ship apart.

Chapter Ten

∾

THERE WAS BLOOD on the floor. Most of it was mine. Some of it was Hollie's. But we were alive. More waves passed above our heads. I felt them tug at the sub as they went over, but they could not take us with them. Outside the hull, the sounds of the old freighter were horrible. I knew she was just a ship, built in a shipyard, and not a living thing, yet the sounds she made as the sea destroyed her were cries and wails of the greatest horror. I didn't think any dying animals' cries could sound worse.

And yet she didn't go down as fast as I thought she would. What was it about this ship that kept her away from the bottom of the sea?

But sinking she was; there was no mistaking that. We listened for hours as the wails went slowly from just beside us, to beneath us, to very slowly dropping farther and farther down. I pulled out the first aid kit and washed my wounds with hydrogen peroxide and bandaged them. There was a cut on my arm where I had once been shot, and the old scar was torn open. There were more bumps on my head. Seeing that Hollie was bleeding from his mouth, I examined him closely to discover if he was bleeding internally or from a cut in his mouth. He was very good at sitting still while I examined him and found the cut in his mouth. He licked it constantly. I looked him over and found a few more bumps, but he seemed pretty good otherwise.

Then I inspected the sub. Other than my things having been thrown around, with spilled oats, sugar, spices, and tea, the sub seemed all right. Ziegfried had designed and built the sub to withstand the worst, and it had. I was amazed and immensely grateful for his foresight.

Only after I had done all these things and settled quietly on my cot, with Hollie on my lap, did I turn my mind to Sensei. I guess I didn't want to think about it. Perhaps I should have rushed back to the surface and searched for him on the water. But I had seen him disappear into the stairwell just seconds before the wave hit. He had probably put his faith in the stability of the ship, which had never failed him before. Whatever the case, I knew I had to accept that he was probably dead. I just didn't want to think about it.

I did have to surface to find Seaweed. He had been outside

when the tsunami struck, but a gigantic wave was not the threat to him that it was to us because he could fly out of its way. I was confident we would find him either flying high in the sky, trying to spot us beneath the surface, or sitting on the water, impatiently wondering where his supper was.

A few hours after the wave struck, we rose to the surface and took a look. The waves were still high, but the tsunami had passed. There was no sign of the ship, not even an oil spill or any debris, which was strange. I opened the hatch. Seaweed dropped out of the sky immediately, gave me one of his displeased looks, and came inside. I raised the binoculars and scanned the water for half an hour but did not find so much as a stick of wood or a plastic cup. Neither were there bubbles coming up from where the ship had gone down. When a ship sinks, water fills her hull and pushes the air out, and the air rises in bubbles to the surface. So I looked for those bubbles, but found none. That made no sense.

I went to the control panel, sat in front of the sonar screen, and searched for the ship. There she was, 133 feet below us. I was surprised she hadn't fallen farther. Her shape was odd because she was upside down. She was level though, not higher in the bow or stern. She must have rolled right over without breaking up. The terrible sounds she had been making were the twisting and bending of metal, but not the tearing. Otherwise she would have filled with water and plummeted to the bottom like a stone.

I stared at the screen hardly blinking; I just couldn't take my eyes away. I wondered if I would watch until she had reached the bottom, two miles down. But the numbers on the screen showed that her depth hadn't changed. Well, it changed a little. It went from 133 feet to 137, to 134, and back to 133. That was unbelievable. It was as if she had hit a floor, and was bouncing. She couldn't be rising; that was a certainty. But why wasn't she sinking?

I watched the screen for an hour. The ship never fell below 137 feet. I made another reconnaissance of the surface directly above her. No bubbles showed. How bizarre. I had to conclude that the plastic Sensei had collected over the years was giving her a neutral buoyancy at around 135 feet, preventing her from falling any deeper. How long could that last? Surely water would find its way inside the holds and everywhere else? Surely it was only a matter of time before she flooded and plunged to the bottom?

Two hours later she was still holding her own at 137 feet below the surface. I didn't know what to think, except for the one thought that kept forcing itself into my head: if the ship had trapped air inside, and Sensei was still on board, then there was a chance he was still alive.

The more I thought about it, the more I realized he probably was. Having hung around him for two weeks, and having observed his extraordinary way of keeping the ship afloat, his amazing garden, his incredible attention to detail, his talent for stealth, and his remarkable ingenuity, it only made sense that he would have anticipated the eventual sinking of the ship. He would have prepared for that by sealing the holds for such an emergency, perhaps even the inner passageways. I didn't know, I was only guessing, but what else could account for the fact that she was not filling with water, as she ought to have?

Yet preventing her from sinking to the bottom was one thing; the point was that she had sunk to 137 feet, and there was no way on earth he could bring her back up, no matter how ingenious he was. So what was his plan? Would he open a door, squeeze out through the water rushing in, and swim up to the surface? It was a long way; he'd have to be able to hold his breath for several minutes. That was possible, I supposed, though I had never seen him holding his breath, just as I had never seen him swim.

But the fact that this was a real possibility created a dilemma for me. On one hand, I wanted to sail to the nearest point of land and go for help. I didn't know how realistic that was either, for lots of reasons, but that was my first thought. On the other hand, if he was going to come out of the ship and swim to the surface, then I needed to stay around to be here for him. Otherwise he'd simply swim around and around in circles until he drowned, that is, if he could even swim. I supposed he could have surfaced with some sort of buoy that would keep him afloat, but unless it was a dinghy in which he could properly rest, and unless it was outfitted with food and water, he'd die of exposure within a week or so.

What should I do: go for help, or stay and wait for him to show up on the surface? I couldn't decide, but it was decided for me simply because I found it impossible to leave. I stayed on the surface, and waited and waited and waited. I searched the water continually for his little head to come bobbing up. But it never did.

As the hours went by, I became less confident that he would ever surface. But why would he wait? Was he preparing something to help him reach the surface? Did he have air tanks hidden somewhere on the ship? I doubted that very much. How would he have filled them? Could he have hidden air compressors where I couldn't find them? That seemed impossible. Besides, he'd need an energy source to fill them.

No, as clever as he was, he just couldn't have hidden a whole bunch of things like that. He would have had to keep a secret room somewhere. Had he? The thought that maybe he had, haunted me. I couldn't know for sure. So I stayed on the surface directly above the ship for nearly a day, a day that could have been spent sailing for help. I did try to reach the Japanese coast guard by shortwave, but kept getting only Japanese voices, all sounding terribly frantic, and I was beginning to wonder if the tsunami had continued all the way to Japan and caused damage there, too. That was a frightening thought.

It was an agonizing day. It kept running through my mind that Sensei was only 137 feet away, less than the length of the ship, and yet we were separated by water, and there was no

way I could reach him. It was tantalizing because I could actually reach the ship with the sub, but once we were there, I
couldn't get out. My absolute maximum free diving depth
was one hundred feet, which was pretty hard to do at the best
of times, and a depth where I couldn't stay for more than a
few seconds. I could hold my breath for four minutes, but it
took more than a minute to get that deep, and the same to
swim back up. The pressure was so heavy down there it was
like an elephant sitting on your chest. Basically, I could only
go down and come back up; I couldn't go down and stay.
And one hundred feet wasn't nearly deep enough anyway.

Then I wondered if I could drop a wrench tied to a rope
onto the hull of the ship, and maybe bang it in a pattern
using Morse code. Did Sensei know Morse code? He might.
So I gathered up my rope, but altogether I could only reach
122 feet. Then I realized I could touch the hull of the ship
with the rope if I swam below fifteen feet.

So I tried that. I tied all my rope together into one piece,
tied it to my heaviest wrench, and went into the water directly below the sub. I swam down and lowered the rope until I felt it stop dropping. It had hit the hull of the ship. I
could feel it but I couldn't hear it. I could still hear sounds
from the ship though, moaning and groaning as if she were
in pain. I raised the rope and tried to lower it, but it dropped
too slowly. I raised it again, hoping to give Sensei the message, "Help is coming." But it took too long to get even the
first word out and I had to surface to grab air. Had Sensei

heard the wrench over the sounds of the ship? I doubted it. It was unlikely he would know from all the other sounds that one of them was me.

And so, one day after the ship went down, I decided my only hope of rescuing Sensei was to go for help. And the closest place to do that was on the mainland of Japan.

Chapter Eleven

⚘

THERE WAS ONE huge problem in leaving to go for help: how would I ever find the ship again? I racked my brain trying to figure it out. Of course I could write down our navigational coordinates, and I did. But the sea is always moving. Mostly the surface travels at about three knots, allowing for wind, which can either push it as fast as five knots, or slow it down. Beneath the surface, the water is also moving, although more slowly. At 137 feet, the sea might be moving at only one or two knots, but it is still moving. To complicate things even more, the water beneath the surface is sometimes moving in a different direction from the water on top.

If a capsized ship drifts at two knots for twenty-four hours, for five days, it will have moved roughly two hundred and fifty nautical miles, which is about two hundred and seventy-five miles on land. And so, even if I came back to the same spot, five days later, the ship would not be here, not even close. And if it took me ten days, she would be twice as far away. But if it took me ten days, Sensei would likely be dead for lack of oxygen. That was another question for which I had no answer: how long could he last on the air he had trapped down there?

If I had enough rope to reach, I could attach some sort of buoy that would drift along with the ship, but the only thing I could think of using for a buoy was the rubber dinghy, which, as big and bright as it seemed to me, would become pretty much invisible once we were out of sight. Trying to find a rubber dinghy, even a bright orange one, on the surface of the ocean, when you are looking at sea level, would be like trying to find a jellybean on a sandy beach. Besides, not only did I not have enough rope to reach, I had no way to tie it to the hull of the ship.

If only I had some sort of tracking device, like the kind they put on sea turtles and whales. But I didn't, so I sat and pondered the problem for hours, unable to help Sensei where we were, yet unable to leave.

The solution finally came, not from me, but from Sensei. And now I knew for sure that he was still alive.

While I was sitting on the hull, staring at the water and

wishing I could go down there, I saw something come up. Like ghostly faces, three yellow plastic bottles tied together made their way to the surface. They didn't come up as fast as buoys normally would because they were attached to a rope. The other end of the rope was attached to the ship. Sensei had somehow opened a door and let this makeshift buoy out. And now I knew that he was alive.

The thought that perhaps he had left the ship, too, with the buoy, and had used it to pull himself to the surface crossed my mind, and I waited to see if he would also appear, alive or dead. But he didn't. He was biding his time. Perhaps he would climb out and use the rope as a guide to the surface. But maybe he wouldn't want to do that until he knew that somebody was actually here. He couldn't know that we had survived the wave too. If he did come to the surface, and there was no one here, he'd have only hours to live, or days, or maybe only minutes if he couldn't swim.

The one thing I could do was dive with the sub and try to gently touch the hull of the ship in such a way as to let Sensei know we were still here. Then perhaps he would leave the ship and try to make it to the surface. That's what I would do if I were him down there, even though I had never felt the pressure at that depth.

On the other hand, I knew that when you were down over a hundred feet in the middle of the sea, it could be quite dark, depending upon what was happening in the sky above, and hard to even know which way was up. You might think it would be obvious but it wasn't. The pressure squeezes against your limbs, and your head feels as if it's in a vice. Moreover, if the sea is dark on the surface, then it's pretty much black at a hundred feet.

Maybe it would be overwhelming holding your breath under such pressure anyway. And maybe the distance was simply too far. I really didn't know. Certainly it would be if you couldn't hold your breath for more than a couple of minutes.

And so, I sealed the hatch, hit the dive switch and we went down. We dove quickly at first, but I pumped a little air into the tanks to slow our descent. As we approached 130 feet, I peered through the observation window, hoping to be able to see the ship, even though the sun did not reach down here.

But I did see her, at least the spooky silhouette of her lying upside down. It was hard to believe that Sensei was down here, just a few feet away on the other side of a wall of water and a wall of steel, and I couldn't reach him.

As gently as possible, I dropped the sub onto the hull of the ship, and there was a bumping and scraping of metal on metal. I couldn't tell if our keel had struck her keel, or her hull. I pumped air into the tanks to rise a few feet, and then let water in to fall. Five times I did this, as rhythmically as possible in the hope that Sensei would hear it and know I was sending him a message. I heard a clanging of metal coming from inside the ship, and it was possible he was banging against the inside wall with a pipe to let me know he understood, but I couldn't know for certain. At least I felt hopeful we had communicated. With that hope I could now go for help.

But when we resurfaced, and I stood in the portal and looked down at the three plastic bottles, I was hit with a feeling of despair. Who was I kidding? I would never find them again. Even if I tied the rubber dinghy to the rope, it would still be no more than a speck on the sea. And though the sea was moving in a certain direction now, it could change its mind at any time, and swing this way or that, and I could be hundreds of miles off track. Wasn't there something else I could do?

It occurred to me that if I could bounce radar waves off the dinghy I'd have a much greater chance of finding it. But how could I do that when the dinghy was made of rubber? I could put a metal plate on the side of it, so that it would reflect radar waves, but since it was sitting right on the surface, the ocean waves would block the radar waves until I was really close, when I'd be able to see it anyway.

But what if I fixed a pole in the centre of the dinghy, and attached a metal plate to it that stuck up eight feet or so? I could test it as we sailed away. That seemed like a good idea. Okay, but I had to hurry. The clock was ticking.

So I removed one of the plated steel doors from the interior wall of the sub—it was fourteen inches square, and weighed about twenty pounds—and I took the gaff, which was seven feet long, and fastened its hook to the plate using small C-clamps. I took my largest steel pot, cut it open with a hacksaw, and hammered it into a thin sheet of shiny metal. I drilled holes through it, and bolted it to the other end of the wooden gaff. Then I wrapped a thick layer of duct tape around the whole length of the pole, to strengthen it. Once outside on the sub, I inflated the dinghy, tied the heavy plate to loops on the floor, and then tied the dinghy securely to the rope that was coming up from the ship.

I stood back on the portal and watched the buoy behave in the breeze. It looked like a stop sign planted in the middle of a giant doughnut, but it tossed and pitched like any other buoy. It would likely reflect a radar signal very imperfectly, but that would be an indication of its location, too, since the signal would be weak and inconsistent, not strong and steady like that of a ship. My radar could detect an object from ten miles at best. Would this makeshift buoy do that? I would find out only as we left the area.

The last thing I did before leaving was to draw a circle with a two-hundred-and-fifty-mile radius out from our coordinates on the map. I drew arrows with a pencil to show the present direction of the current. The current would likely change, and one thing was certain: the dinghy and the ship would not be where they were right now. This was a very rough method for finding something at sea, but it was the best I could do.

Though I was not very religious, I said a prayer for Sensei as I cranked up the engine and pulled away. Seaweed sat on the bow for the first while as we ploughed through the waves heading west. Hollie stood in the portal with me, looking back towards the spot where his new friend remained.

"Don't worry, Hollie. We're coming back for him."

He looked at me to see if I was telling the truth. He knew the difference.

"We are. I promise."

The metal sheet behaved more or less as I thought it would: it gave a decent signal while we were in sight of it, but the farther we sailed away, the weaker it became. As the dinghy spun around in the water, the sheet would present either a flat surface, a paper-thin edge, or something in between, and its signal would reflect that. From five miles the signal was fair, not great. From eight, it wasn't very good, although it was still occasionally there. As we were leaving our radar reach, there was no sign of it at all. I took a deep breath. We were going to have to rely on hope now. That was all we had.

Chapter Twelve

✍

IN THE TWO WEEKS I spent on the ship, we had drifted mostly in a northeasterly direction, occasionally correcting our course with the makeshift sails, and travelling probably a thousand miles. It seemed hard to believe that any floating object, either ship or plastic cup, could drift so far in that time, but the sea is the largest body on Earth, and it likes to move around. Looking at our coordinates now, I figured the closest land we could reach was the port of Choshi, on the mainland of Japan, not far from the city of Tokyo. Choshi was about two hundred and seventy-five miles away. We could reach it in little more than half a day, at top speed, with any luck.

Well, that turned out to be wishful thinking. It took an agonizing twenty-one hours to reach the coast. The current and wind pushed against us all the way. I didn't dare sail on the surface for the last twelve miles, which, by the Law of the Sea, was Japan's territorial zone, where we were much more likely to be spotted on radar, or by another vessel. So we sailed in at periscope depth, while I waited and waited for a suitable ship to follow into the harbour. There were a few vessels coming in and out of the port, but we needed to find one that could hide us beneath it perfectly.

Impatiently, I waited two miles offshore for almost three hours, until I spotted a small tanker turning in towards the port. I submerged to fifty feet, snuck in underneath her, and followed her in. With the pounding of her engines right above our heads, it was so loud it made my teeth rattle. Seaweed sat with a dark frown, and Hollie buried his head in his paws, but at least we were able to enter the harbour undetected.

I had to be extremely careful visiting Japan. Not only would Japanese authorities consider us a threat, being an unknown submarine coming in illegally, they would almost certainly recognize us from news footage from the Southern Ocean. A few months earlier we had helped the Sea Shepherd Society prevent a tanker from refueling Japanese whaling ships. I had also been accused of sabotaging a Japanese tanker in the port of Perth, Australia, which I didn't do, but they didn't know that. They would consider me a criminal of the worst kind, lock me up, and throw away the key.

I had never planned to come to such a highly populated part of the country. I would have avoided the mainland of Japan altogether, and maybe just visited the quiet island of Okinawa, a thousand miles south. Now I didn't have much choice; I had to seek help wherever I could get it, and try not to worry too much about the risk. I just could not get caught.

Beneath the tanker, the only way to know where we were was by sonar pictures of the sea floor below and the sound of the engines above. The sea floor kept rising as we approached the coast, but the tanker's engines didn't cut out until the last minute, which was pretty strange. Wouldn't she cut her engines when the tugboats came out to meet her? I listened hard for the sound of tugboats, but it never came. Neither did the tanker cut her engines completely. That was crazy, too. Was she planning to run aground? The sea floor had risen a lot, and we must have been right outside the harbour. It was unnerving not being able to see. What the heck was going on?

I had to know before we ran into something ourselves, so I shut off the batteries, dropped behind the tanker, and rose to take a peek. As I raised the periscope and looked through the lens, I realized there was no harbour. There was only a breakwater, and, to the right of that, the opening of a river. That was where the tanker was headed, on her own power. It would take an awfully skilled pilot to make that turn around the breakwater and enter the river, but that was exactly what

the tanker did. And we followed her in. Once inside the shel-
tered water, I let the tanker sail away from us and searched
for a place to moor out of sight.

That, at least, was easy. Inside the marina were many
berths for ships, and they were mostly empty. In fact, I saw
only two small ships, which looked like coast guard vessels,
and they were tied up, lights out, sitting as quiet as moths. It
was late afternoon, but with the exception of the ship we had
followed in, I didn't see any more movement on the water. It
was a small industrial-looking marina. While it wasn't old, it
looked more or less abandoned. That was strange, too.

Though we had to be careful, we didn't have the luxury of
wasting time. Every hour we took here was an hour less air
Sensei had to breathe. I tried not to obsess about that, but it
was hard not to.

Still, we had to wait until dark, which was two hours away.
I couldn't go marching across the bridge from the breakwater and through the dockyard in daylight. I would have to
sneak across in the dark, like a ninja.

I chose one of the smallest berths that jutted out from the
breakwater, tucked the sub into the corner, and waited for
two hours. I spent that time cooking rice and beans, fed the
crew an extra-large serving, and put out extra food and water
for them. I didn't plan on taking anything with me except
some money in my pocket. I wanted to travel as light as possible. If I did get caught, I would tell the authorities exactly
where the sub was, and that there was a dog inside, and just

hope they would find a home for him. I let Seaweed out. He could survive anywhere.

Once it was dark, I rose until the hatch was barely an inch above the surface. I climbed out and tied up to the rocks. There were no lights on the breakwater. I went back inside, gave Hollie a pat and a fresh piece of rope to chew, and told him to wait for me. I changed my shorts for a pair of pants, put on my jacket, and pulled my hat down to hide that I was not Japanese. Then I climbed out, shut the hatch, and crept across the causeway to the dockyard.

The causeway led to a small open yard, and a few small warehouses. It looked like an industrial fishing dockyard. It wasn't fancy, and I doubted there were any cameras. There didn't seem to be any people either, but I couldn't take the chance, so I stayed in the shadows.

As I looked around beneath the few streetlights here and there, I saw large piles of junk that had been bulldozed into the corners such as you would find at a landfill. Sitting silently in the dark were half a dozen bulldozers. The piles contained tires, wood, broken pieces of metal, plastic, bottles, buoys, rocks, and seaweed. The tsunami had struck here, I realized, though it must not have struck too hard because even the smallest buildings close to the water looked completely intact. I didn't see broken windows or doors. There wasn't much damage, it seemed, just a big mess. No doubt the large breakwater was the main reason. It had broken the tsunami's back before it could destroy the town.

But what about coastal towns without a large breakwater?

The industrial zone was wide but not very deep. It came to a sudden end at a small woods. There, I climbed a tree. It had been a long time since I climbed a tree, and I was surprised how easy it was and how much stronger I felt after just two weeks of training with Sensei.

From the treetop I saw a small city of houses and buildings, with few streetlights, and very few neon signs. It was eerily quiet. I had no idea which way to go, so I tried to memorize the shape of the city before climbing down from the tree. I was looking for a dive shop where I could rent scuba gear in the morning, and maybe even hire someone to help me. Asking the coast guard for help would have been a lot better, but that was not an option.

It wasn't that late but there was no one in the streets. Nobody. After ten streets or so, I still hadn't seen a single person. Where was everyone? There were lights in the houses, so I knew there were people here. But why wasn't anyone out in the streets? Neither did I see any cars. Finally, after almost two hours, I spotted a little old woman hurrying down a street. Even though it was warm out, she was heavily dressed, wearing a kerchief over her head, and a mask over her face. I knew it was a woman by the way she scurried along. As she was moving pretty fast for an old woman, I had to run to catch up. When she crossed a street, and stood waiting for a red light to turn green, even though there were no cars coming, I caught up to her.

I startled her. I didn't mean to. She said something urgently in Japanese, then covered her mask with a gloved hand. I had no idea what she was trying to tell me. Then she did it again, more urgently, as if I were doing something terribly wrong. I questioned her with my eyes. She shook her head angrily. Then she reached into her coat pocket, pulled out another face mask, and handed it to me. She kept saying one word over and over: "Fukushima! Fukushima!" But I had no idea what that was. She insisted so strongly that I take the mask, that I did. Then she bowed slightly and rushed away, around a corner and into a small apartment building. I wanted to follow and ask if she knew where a dive shop was, but figured I'd have a better chance asking somebody else. I put the mask in my pocket and kept going.

Most of the houses and buildings were small and very plain—just flat boxes with square windows and flat roofs. But some were curved, with tall rectangular windows and curled roofs with red clay tiles. Some even had dragon heads on the corners of their roofs, which were very cool. Most had lights on inside, but were dimly lit, as if they were trying to save energy. All of the houses had slat blinds in the windows, and, like the streets, were neat and tidy, except where piles of rubbish from the tsunami had been swept into corners and had not yet been picked up.

I searched and searched but could not find a dive shop. Neither could I find an open restaurant, or even a pizzeria! I might as well have been looking on the moon. What the heck was going on? The tsunami had struck days ago; surely there was nothing to fear now?

Finally I walked in front of a TV shop, and though it was closed, there were screens on in the windows. All of the TVs were showing the news, and the news was the same: pictures of buildings by the ocean that looked like large factories or chemical plants. I saw signs for radioactivity. Most of the writing was in Japanese, but there were a few words occasionally in English at the bottom of the screens. I saw the word "Fukushima" over and over. That was the word the old woman had said. The news showed workers standing around in special suits, like space suits, watching the buildings, but not going inside. "Fukushima. Fukushima . . ." the TVs repeated.

As I continued staring at the screens I started to wonder if something more than the tsunami had happened. The screens switched to a city on the shore, where they showed buildings being flattened by the sea, with cars, trucks, and even ships being washed right into the streets. The tsunami had struck some cities very hard. Even though it had happened a couple of days earlier, they were still showing the footage constantly. I stood mesmerized by the destruction. Hundreds of cars and vans were being swept around like empty tin cans in a sewer drain. Large industrial fishing boats were lying on their sides or heaved right on top of buildings. It was unbelievable to see.

People were clinging to the roofs of their houses that were

being swept away, and bodies were shown strewn across beaches. I couldn't believe it. All of this had happened very close to here, although Choshi had been spared.

But the news kept repeating the words, "Fukushima . . . Fukushima . . ." And then . . . "*Nuclear Meltdown.*" I froze. As bad as a tsunami was, I had the feeling a nuclear catastrophe might be much worse. Now I knew why the old woman had been wearing the mask. I felt my skin crawl as if there were tiny spiders all over it.

Chapter Thirteen

I REACHED INTO my pocket and put the mask on my face. I pulled the collar of my jacket tighter around my neck. Now I knew why the people here were staying in their houses. They were trying not to breathe in radioactive air. I couldn't help breathing it in. Two minutes ago, the air seemed normal to me. Now I was afraid it would kill me. Would it kill me? Everything I had ever read about radiation was bad.

I stared at the map on the TV. Fukushima was about two hundred miles north. Maybe here the air wasn't so bad. Maybe I would be okay. As I stared at the screens I realized I had to make a decision. I could run away now, hoping that I hadn't been too badly poisoned, and let Sensei die, or I could keep searching for help here and try to rescue him, knowing that I'd probably be sicker in the long run.

It wasn't an easy decision because I was really scared. I didn't want to get cancer. I didn't want my lungs to fail. I was too young to fall seriously ill, too young to die. Sensei was already very old.

I didn't know what to do, so I shut my eyes and tried to centre myself the way we did when we were meditating, and waited for the answer to come from inside. And slowly it came. None of us lives forever. There's not even any guarantee we'll live to be old, like Sensei. We're lucky if we do. What was more important to me was not how long I lived, but that I lived a life I could feel proud of. If I ran away and let Sensei die, I didn't think I could ever feel proud of myself again. I didn't think I would even be able to look in the mirror again.

Well, that settled that.

But where were the dive shops? There had to be dive shops in a port city? I went up and down the streets faster and faster, until I was sweating. The mask on my face was dripping, and I was breathing in poisonous air the whole time. Still I found nothing. What should I do? Should I bang on someone's door and beg for help? But how could they help me unless they were divers? And how could I know that they wouldn't just turn me in to the police?

Four hours after leaving the sub, I had been up and down dozens of streets. I had seen shops for cameras, books, paper, electronics, furniture, marine devices, medical devices, teaching aids, musical instruments, food, toys, and clothing, but not a single shop that sold scuba gear! Sweating like a pig, I felt I had to take off my jacket, hat, and mask. But the moment I did, another old woman appeared out of nowhere and screamed at me to put them back on. She slapped her arms, and gestured for me to cover up. "*Fukushima!*" she cried. "*Fukushima!*" Her eyes were filled with fear.

"Okay! Okay!" So I put them back on. Then I tried to ask the old woman where I could find a dive shop, but she ran away, and I didn't try to chase her; she was already too upset. This was crazy! I was getting nowhere.

I had to stop rushing around. I had to stop sweating or dehydration would drain all of my energy. There just *had* to be something I could do.

As I went down one dead-end street, close to the edge of the woods, I noticed in the very last house a martial arts studio on the second floor. There was a sign that showed two men fighting with swords. It reminded me of Sensei, and I stopped below the sign and stared at it. Maybe somebody who respected ninjas would be willing to help me rescue Sensei, or at least tell me where there was a dive shop.

So I went to the door and knocked. Nobody answered. I knocked again, more loudly. No one came to the door. Was there anyone home? There were no lights on. I stared down the street from where I had come. In the other direction was the woods. I was tired and frustrated and feeling desperate.

If there was anyone in that studio, I wanted to find them.

There was a high fence around the house and yard; the only way to get to the back of the house was to climb it. Sensei could have jumped right over it without touching it. I had to jump onto the fence, pull myself up, and swing my legs over and down into the yard. Except for a few tiny bug lights next to a garden, it was very dark. There were no lights on at the back of the house either, but I did see a tiny light coming from the studio above.

The second floor had a balcony but no way to get up there. Once again, Sensei could have jumped to it. But I wasn't Sensei. Like a beginning student of ninjutsu, I climbed the drainpipe that came down one corner of the house until I could grip the underside of the balcony floor with my hands. Then I swung myself into the air and hung there for a moment, trying to figure out what to do next. I kicked off my sneakers, and then started to swing back and forth to gain momentum. The balcony creaked with my weight, but my feet reached a space at one edge; now I was gripping with both my hands and feet. Crawling upside down beneath the balcony floor, I came to one corner, and then pulled myself up onto the top. I jumped down into the balcony as quietly as I could, and crept over to the door. I felt like a ninja now.

Through the window I saw a small light that looked like a candle. I pressed my face up against the glass and got a fright. On the other side of the glass was another face staring back at me in absolute terror.

I forced myself to smile, but it didn't do any good; the terror on the other side of the glass just got worse. I heard a scream. It sounded young, and I think the person on the other side of the glass was younger than me. Suddenly the blind moved, and I saw another face, a bigger, fatter face, and it didn't look frightened; it looked angry. I tried harder to smile and waved with my hand in a friendly way. "Can you help me?"

A minute later, the door slid sideways and a man stepped out. He was holding a sword in his hands. Right away, he reminded me of Sensei, not only because of his sword, but the way he was standing, with his feet wide apart and his knees slightly bent. He was ready to fight. I wasn't afraid though, because he looked like a gentle man, and I was unarmed. I felt confident he wouldn't attack an unarmed man. A boy about ten years old took a step outside the door and stood behind him.

"Who are you? What do you want?" said the man. He had a sharp Japanese accent but I was glad he spoke English.

"I am sorry to bother you," I said. "I need help."

The man's face softened immediately, but he still looked suspicious. "Why do you need help? Are you sick? Why are you outside? Don't you know there is contamination?"

"Yes. I know. I am not sick, but my friend needs help. He is trapped inside a ship. I need to find a dive shop where I can rent scuba gear. I cannot find one in your city. Do you know where there is a dive shop?"

I spoke slowly, and the man listened carefully to everything I said. He thought about it for a while before he answered.

"Where are you from?"

"Canada."

"How did you get here?"

"I sailed here."

"Do you have a boat?"

"I have a submarine." Normally I wouldn't tell people that, but I knew that if I hoped to win his help, I'd have to earn his trust. And I'd do that better if I told him the truth.

"The man I need to rescue is an old man."

"How old?"

"A hundred years old."

He made a strange face. I wasn't sure he believed that, but I was being completely honest with him, and I think he could feel it.

"He is a ninja," I said, hoping that would make a difference.

It did. The man's face went pale. He just stood and stared at me with a kind of shocked expression. Then he slid open the door. "These are strange days. Please come inside."

So I followed them into the studio, which was in the back of their apartment. There were a few small candles lit with mats on the floor. "Come in," repeated the man, and he led me through the studio into the front of the apartment where there were two very small bedrooms, a kitchen, and a small living room. It was clean and tidy. "I am Yoshi," he said. "This is Katsuo." He pointed to the boy. I couldn't tell if he was his son, or his younger brother. "Would you like some tea?"

"Yes, thank you very much." I was dying of thirst.

While I sat at the small wooden table, Yoshi put a kettle on the stove, prepared a teapot with loose tea, and put out three small cups. He didn't speak until the tea was ready. The boy just sat on the other chair, staring at me the whole time. Finally, when the tea had steeped, Yoshi poured us each a cup, sat down, and stared into my face with great curiosity. "Please. Tell me about this old man."

So I did. First, I explained who I was, where I had come from, and why I had come to Japan. I told him everything, hoping that if I were completely honest, he would want to help me. Then I explained how I had come upon the old freighter, met Sensei, and how the tsunami had capsized and sunk the ship. Lastly, I explained what I was hoping to do.

"Amazing," said Yoshi, when I was finished. "Do you know there is a legend about an old ninja who sails the sea on a ghost ship?"

"No, I didn't know that."

"I have grown up with this story. But you have seen him. Everything you say is true to the legend, except that the ship is said to be a ghost ship. Did you see ghosts?"

"No."

"And the old man, do you think he is really one hundred years old?"

"Yes, I think so."

"*Sensei* means teacher. I am a sensei of martial art. So that is not the old man's name. He was just telling you that he is your teacher."

"He was my teacher. Do you know if there are any dive shops here?"

Yoshi shook his head. "No. There are no dive shops in Choshi. But I have a friend who dives. Maybe he will help you."

"Do you think so? Do you think you could ask him?"

"I can ask him tomorrow."

I felt a sudden panic. "Tomorrow will be too late! Is there any way you could ask him tonight? It is very important that I go back as soon as possible because Sensei will run out of air."

Yoshi thought it over. "He won't like it, but maybe we can ask him tonight."

"I can give you some money."

"No. No money. But my friend . . . he might like your money."

"Okay."

"You are very determined to save this old man."

"Yes."

"Did you know that thousands of people have died in the tsunami?"

"Thousands?"

"Yes. Many more will die now because of radioactive

poison. Maybe everyone will die. This is the worst thing that has ever happened. This is why you see no one in the street. Maybe you would be wiser to leave now. Maybe your old friend is already dead."

"I think he is still alive."

"The legend says that he is a ghost. Maybe he brought the tsunami. Do you think so?"

"No. He is just an old man."

Chapter Fourteen

ONCE OUTSIDE, I collected my sneakers and followed Yoshi through the streets to his friend's house. Katsuo wanted to come, but Yoshi said no. We wore our jackets, hats and masks pulled tight. Yoshi wore gloves. I kept my hands in my pockets.

We went quickly, and didn't talk along the way so we wouldn't have to breathe as much. I was happy that Yoshi was trusting me. It gave me hope. I tried to imagine Sensei sitting inside the ship, in darkness. Was he meditating? Was he sleeping? Was he staying calm? Was he still alive, and would he still be alive when I got there? I wouldn't know until I did.

After about half an hour we reached another house, went through a side gate, and Yoshi knocked loudly on the door. No one answered. "He doesn't like to answer his door," said Yoshi. He knocked again and again, more loudly, until the door finally opened, and a bigger man stuck his head out and said something in Japanese with an angry voice. Then he saw Yoshi, and a great smile replaced his angry look. They embraced, and the man questioned Yoshi with a soft, sweet voice. They spoke in Japanese, and the man stared at me on and off. I smiled and tried to look like somebody he could trust, but didn't know if it was working. Finally he insisted we come in.

His name was Hitoshi. He didn't speak English well, but he could understand it a little. Yoshi explained everything to him while we sat on cushions on the floor. Once in a while Yoshi said a word I understood, like "ninja" or "sensei," and Hitoshi's eyes opened wide. He asked Yoshi a bunch of excited questions that were probably about the legend they had both grown up with. Towards the end, Yoshi asked him a few pointed questions, and waited for a response between each one, but mostly Hitoshi was shaking his head, which didn't look good. Finally Yoshi nodded in understanding, thanked Hitoshi, and turned to me. He had a sympathetic look on his face.

"He cannot help you because you are wanted by the police. He saw you on TV. If he is caught helping you, he will go to prison too, and there will be no one left to look after his parents. He must be here to look after his parents. He is very sorry. He hopes you understand."

I felt crushed. I looked at Hitoshi and saw his apologetic face. I nodded that I understood. "Can he tell me where I can get scuba gear? Would he let me borrow his?"

Yoshi spoke to Hitoshi again, then answered me. "He has scuba gear, but he cannot help you. He is very sorry."

"Does he know where else I might be able to get some?"

"No one will want to help you because you are a criminal. I don't think it will be possible for you to get any scuba gear. Hitoshi wants to know if you saw the old ninja jump. Could he jump over walls?"

I stared at Hitoshi. I felt a little angry because he wouldn't help, angry that there was a justice system that wasn't really just. I was believed to be a criminal just because I had tried to stop people from killing whales, the most beautiful creatures on the planet. I felt so angry inside, but I knew that I couldn't show that now. I had to try to win these guys over to help me. "Yes, he can jump over walls. He can jump eight feet into the air."

"Did you see him do it with your own eyes?"

"Yes."

Hitoshi smiled like a little boy, and his eyes watered with excitement. But he would not help me.

Such a feeling of desperation rose up inside of me. I asked Hitoshi if I could just see his scuba gear. He frowned. "You want to see it?" said Yoshi.

"If you don't mind. I have never scuba dived before. I have done a lot of free diving. I can hold my breath for four minutes and dive to one hundred feet."

Yoshi nodded his head towards Hitoshi. They were impressed with that.

"Scuba diving: is it difficult?"

Hitoshi frowned, and answered in very broken English. "Not . . . difficult, but . . . no mistake. Follow rules . . . not difficult . . . but . . . no mistake."

"Do you have a book about it?" I asked.

Hitoshi nodded.

Yoshi and I followed Hitoshi into a basement room where I saw several tanks, masks, snorkels, fins, and wet suits lying around on the floor. Hitoshi was not clean and tidy like Yoshi. He went to a small bookshelf and pulled out a book that had lost its cover. He handed it to me. One part was in Japanese, one in German, one in Spanish, one in French, and one in English. He opened it to a page with tables.

"Follow rules . . . or . . . many sickness."

I glanced at the page. I read the word, *Narcosis*. "What is narcosis?"

"Like . . . very drunk," said Yoshi. "Hitoshi says you must take a scuba diving course . . . or you die."

"I understand. Can I at least borrow this book?"

Yoshi asked Hitoshi. Hitoshi shrugged, and handed me the book.

"Thank you. I promise I will never tell anyone where I got it," I said.

Hitoshi looked genuinely sorry. Then, just before we left the room, he went to a small window at the top of the wall. I watched as he reached up and unlocked it. He turned and said something to Yoshi. Yoshi relayed it to me. "Hitoshi says that it is not his fault if he is robbed."

"What?" I wasn't sure I understood what I had just heard. But the two men dropped their heads, and would not say any more.

Chapter Fifteen

ON THE WAY BACK to Yoshi's house I paid close attention to the streets so that I could find my way back to Hitoshi's. I had been invited to rob him. That's what he meant. No other explanation made any sense. Why would he have unlocked the window while I was there, and said what he said? I guess it was the only way to give me what I needed, while still protecting himself. He could then honestly declare he had not helped me, that he had, in fact, been robbed.

But I had to rob him. And I wasn't looking forward to that.

It wasn't easy to memorize the way because so many of the streets looked the same to me. But there was one house with dragons on the corners of the fence, and once I found that on my return, I'd know I was close.

Yoshi did not speak on the way back, but I think he was feeling badly that Hitoshi could offer me help only in this weird way. There was one more thing I had to ask Yoshi: could I use his telephone to make a long-distance call? I would reverse the charges of course. He thought about it for a while, and I was afraid he was going to say no, but he said yes.

When we got back, he led me into the small kitchen where his telephone was. While he went into another room with Katsuo, I made a call to Ziegfried and Sheba.

Sheba picked up the phone on the other side of the world. She was like a mother to me. The older I got, the more I felt that. As I heard her loving voice come through the phone, I pictured her standing in the kitchen of her home, on her own little island in Bonavista Bay, Newfoundland, and my heart began to thump with emotion. I wanted to be there now, and sit down with her and Ziegfried at the kitchen table to drink tea and talk about my travels, to hear everything that was new in their lives.

They were married now. I had seen them in India, where they travelled for their honeymoon. But now they were back home, surrounded by the animals and birds and plants they lived with, on their tiny island in the sea. They were the very best people in the whole world, and I missed them so much.

I found it difficult to speak without my voice breaking.

Sheba had a way of stripping away all my defences just with the sound of her voice.

"Alfred! I am so happy to hear from you! Happy Birthday to you! How I wish we could have shared it with you. Where are you, my darling boy? How are you? Are you eating well? Are you safe? When are you coming home? You should be here now already. We miss you so much. The cats miss you. The dogs miss you. The goats and birds miss you. Please tell me you are on your way home now."

I took a deep breath and tried to answer without my voice cracking. "I am okay. I miss you, too. I wish I were there. I am coming home as soon as I can. I am in Japan right now."

"Japan?"

I could hear the fear in Sheba's voice now, and there was a long pause, which told me she was sharing the news about Japan with Ziegfried. I could picture the two of them standing in the kitchen—Ziegfried, as tall and wide as a tree, and Sheba, tall and thin, with her beautiful long red hair and its thousands of wave-like curls. There would be cats all over the kitchen, and birds on top of the fridge, and Edgar the goat standing by the wood stove, with his sleepy sad eyes and goatee beard.

"But why are you in Japan, my dear? Don't you know of the earthquake and tsunami, and the meltdown of the nuclear plants? It is so terrible."

"Yes, I do. I am here to get help for someone, and then I will leave. I am fine, really I am."

There was a long pause. I knew they were discussing things, and I knew that Ziegfried would be anxious to talk to me. I needed to talk to him.

"Alfred, you *must* leave right away. It is terrible what is happening. You must leave, or you will become terribly ill. It is all in the news. Please leave right away. Please tell me that you will."

"I will. I promise. I just need to get help for someone."

"Yes, you are always helping someone. Why does that not surprise me? I had once thought that you were just a young explorer, a most courageous one, but I know now that you are actually a warrior for peace. You have gone out into the world to give help where it is needed. Do you know that I am so proud of you?"

"I guess so."

"We will wait for you then, darling boy, but you must promise me you will leave Japan immediately. Not a moment later."

"I will. I promise. Do you think I could speak with Ziegfried, too?"

"Yes, yes, of course. He is here, jumping up and down waiting for me to hand you over to him." Sheba laughed. "He is more of a boy than you are. He is such a boy." She laughed again. "But he is anxious to speak to you also, so I will pass you over to him. My heart sails with you, my dear Alfred. My heart sails always with you. And I miss you."

"I miss you, too."

"Please remember at all times, our young warrior for peace, that virtue is its own reward."

"What? Okay."

"Will you remember that?"

"Yes, I will."

I found it odd for her to say that to me just then, but I put it away in the back of my mind for later. I took a deep breath when she passed the phone over, and there was another pause. I was pleased I had managed to keep my voice from shaking too much, and glad that Sheba had not read my cards, or dreamt about me, because, with what I was planning to do, I wouldn't have wanted to know what she would have discovered.

When Ziegfried came to the phone, it was completely different. It was like shifting from your heart to your mind. I loved Ziegfried every bit as much as Sheba, but where she was loving and gentle, he was logical and practical. In some ways they were probably the perfect match. She was like a poet, and he was like a scientist. Being around the two of them at the same time was sheer magic.

On the phone Ziegfried was all practicality. If you didn't know that behind his voice there was a warm and loving face, you might sometimes think you were talking to a drill sergeant in the army.

"Al. Sheba says you are in Japan."

"Yes. I just got here, but I'm leaving right away."

"Good. Get out of there immediately. It's a dangerous place, Al. Try to stay indoors. Try to avoid the air."

"Okay."

"Why are you there? Didn't you hear about the tsunami?"

"Yes, I saw it."

"You saw it?"

"Yes."

"Were you hit by it?"

"Yes, but I'm okay. The sub is okay."

"Are you certain? Have you checked for leaks? Yes, of course you have checked for leaks, but are you certain she is all right? Are you certain she is still seaworthy?"

"I'm certain she is. But I need to help somebody else who is trapped in a ship that went down. That's why I'm here. I need to get scuba gear and go and help him."

There was a long pause.

"Ziegfried?"

Now his voice changed. And right from the beginning I didn't like the sound of it.

"Lay it out for me, Al. Tell me everything. Be as detailed as you can, and try not to leave anything out. I'll interrupt you only when I need to know a specific detail."

"Okay." So I did. I started at the very beginning, describing as much as I could, as quickly as I could. Ziegfried interrupted only a few times, such as when I told him Sensei's age, or how high he could jump, or the depth the freighter was sitting at, or how many holds she had, and how big they were. It took such a long time that I was tired when I finished. The weight of carrying Sensei's life in my hands was wearing me out. But when I finally finished, stopped to catch my breath, and waited to hear Ziegfried's response, there wasn't one, just another long pause.

"Ziegfried?"

"I'm thinking, Al."

So I waited. But it felt like forever. And when Ziegfried finally did respond, his words were very difficult to hear.

"Al?"

"Yes?"

"Al. He's a hundred years old. Or so you think."

"I think he is."

"You just turned seventeen."

"I know."

"Al. This is not going to be easy for you to accept."

"What?"

"You have to let him go."

"What? What do you mean?" I was shocked.

"You have to let him go."

"What do you mean, 'let him go'? Do you mean not try to *save* him?"

"Yes. That's exactly what I mean."

Chapter Sixteen

❧

I DIDN'T THINK I was hearing clearly. "I don't understand. Are you saying I shouldn't go back there and try to save him?"

"Yes, that's what I'm saying."

"But . . . he's a wonderful old man. And he's in great shape. I don't get it." I was really upset.

"Al. Let's say he really is a hundred years old, and let's say he is in incredible shape, as you say he is. I have no doubt that is true. Even so, it would be highly unlikely that he'd make it to a hundred and ten, in the best of circumstances."

"But—"

"People just don't live that long, Al. There might be a handful of people on the Earth who have lived that long."

"So?"

"You've got your whole life ahead of you. He has lived his life. The risks you are considering taking are simply too great. Chances are that neither of you would come out of it alive; that's simply a risk I cannot let you take. It's not right, Al. It's not fair. It would be different if he were a lot younger, you know? Even then it's debatable whether the risk would be worth it; it seems like a pretty slim shot to me. And you'd be throwing your life away in the remote hope of saving someone who has already lived more than most people ever dream of living, and who in the very best scenario might live a few more years, that is, if he is still alive. You must consider that all you might find is a floating corpse. It's just not a fair trade, Al."

"But . . . " I didn't like what I was hearing. Even more, I didn't like that it was Ziegfried who was saying it. I was struggling not to feel betrayed. In my mind's eye I saw Sensei sitting inside the hull, in the dark, breathing less than a human normally needs to breathe because he has slowed his pulse and is saving his energy. He's conserving it all in an act to survive. And there is only one possible hope that he will survive: if I go back.

"Al . . . ? Al . . . ?"

"Yes?"

"Let me ask you something."

"Okay."

"What would you think if you saw two other people caught

in this situation: an old man in the very final years of his life, and a young man full of purpose, with his whole life ahead of him? What would you advise, knowing that chances were the young man would not come out of it—that neither the young man nor the old man would come out of it. What would you advise: to let both perish, or to save the one you knew you could save?"

I tried to think about it. That seemed different to me. My mind was beginning to understand what Ziegfried was saying, but my heart wouldn't accept it.

"What would you advise, Al?"

Now it was my turn to pause for a long time before answering.

"I don't know."

"Al?"

"Yes?"

"You and I have an agreement."

Oh, no! I knew what he was going to say.

"We have an agreement, right?"

"Yes."

"We have an agreement that you get to decide where to sail your sub, and you can sail it all over the world as you do, right?"

"Right."

"But that I have the right to ground the sub whenever I feel that you are not safe, right? . . . Right? . . . Al. Answer me."

"Yes. Right. We do."

"I'm sorry, Al, I really and truly am, but I am now officially grounding the sub . . . "

"*What?* No!"

"She's grounded, Al. She's grounded. I'm sorry."

"No!"

"I'm going to send you a plane ticket, Al. You are exhausted, and you are in a dangerous place. I'll send you a ticket. They don't know who you are. They don't know your name . . . Just change your appearance."

"No . . . "

"You're worn out. I can hear it in your voice. You're in a country that is flooding with radioactive particles. A large part of the population is getting sick. It's not safe where you are, Al. You need to come home and rest. You can leave the sub on the bottom of a harbour somewhere; we can come back for it at another time. And if we can't find her, we'll build another one. It's time to come home, Al. It's time to come home."

The strain of all the pressure and the strain of the disappointment I was now feeling were too much for me and I started to cry. I just couldn't help it.

"I can't come home. I can't leave Hollie and Seaweed behind." I rubbed the tears from my eyes but couldn't keep my voice from breaking. "What if I meet you in Okinawa. Would that be okay?"

There was another pause.

"Would that be okay? Ziegfried?"

"Okinawa?"

"Yes. We could sail there in just a few days. And if you could come, then we could refit the sub enough for me to sail it home. Don't you think that could work?"

"I don't know, Al."

"I could rest up there."

"Let me look at the map."

"Okay."

I took a deep breath and wiped my eyes. Katsuo was staring at me from the doorway. I frowned and tried hard to get my emotions under control.

"Al?"

"Yes?"

"Okay. I will meet you in Okinawa. It's pretty far away from the mainland; it should be safe enough. But you've got to get out of there now. You must leave right away. Okay?"

"I will. I promise."

"And, Al?"

"Yes."

"You have to let the old man go."

I didn't answer.

"It's exceedingly unlikely he's still alive, Al. You must accept that."

"Yeah."

"I need to hear you say it, Al."

"Say what?"

"That you will not attempt this rescue; that you will honour our agreement. I need to hear you promise me that you will honour the agreement we made three years ago. I need to hear you say it."

"I will."

"Say it, Al. Then I will know that we understand each other."

"I will honour our agreement."

"And you will not attempt this rescue."

"I will not attempt this rescue."

"Okay, Al. I'll book a flight to Japan right away. I'll try to get there by next week. Shouldn't be too difficult to do that; I don't imagine too many people are flying to Japan right now. Call Sheba as soon as you get to Okinawa, okay? She'll tell you where to meet me. For now, let's say we'll meet in a week's time on the northern tip of Okinawa. There's a place called Cape Heda. I'll meet you there on the beach, or the cliff, or whatever is there, okay?"

"Okay."

"And if either of us can't make it for any reason, we'll get in touch through Sheba, okay?"

"Okay."

"All right, Al. Now, please get inside the sub and get the heck out of there."

"I will. I will right away."

"Good. We're thinking of you, Al. We send you all our love."

"I love you, too."

After I hung up I rubbed my face and tried to shake the emotion out of my head. Katsuo kept staring at me as if I were some sort of secret agent, but Yoshi looked sympathetic. He didn't try to hide that he had overheard me and that I was upset. He gripped my arm when I thanked him for the use of the phone. I made my way towards the door.

"Sometimes we must accept what we don't want to accept," he said. "I know what this is like."

I nodded my head and stared into his face. He was a very kind man. I wondered if Sensei had been anything like him when he was his age.

Chapter Seventeen

ॐ

IT WAS AFTER MIDNIGHT when I wandered back to the dockyard. At every step I felt a weight on my shoulders. My loyalty to Ziegfried was rock solid. He had believed in me at the most important time in my life; it was because of him that I was not pulling lobster and crab from the sea with my grandfather. Without Ziegfried I would never have met Hollie, Seaweed, or Sheba. I would never have sailed the world in my own submarine. I would only have known the sea from the side of a fishing boat, day after day, with my cranky old grandfather nagging me for not doing everything exactly right. I loved my grandfather, but he *was* cranky and impossible to please. Ziegfried helped me escape that life, and I could never forget that.

So, in a way, it wasn't really my decision. *I* wasn't abandoning Sensei; I was just obeying the order of the only one who had the right to give me an order. So it was out of my hands. Probably Sensei *was* dead now, as Ziegfried had suggested. It would be wrong to throw my life away trying to rescue him, especially when I had never scuba dived before, didn't know what I was doing, and would almost certainly kill myself, and maybe Sensei, too, if he wasn't already dead.

As I continued towards the dockyard, I tried to accept it, and put a good face on it, or at least one I could live with. And, for a little while, I actually did. I raised my head and looked around and picked up my pace. Hollie and Seaweed were waiting for me. I would join them inside the sub and we would head for Okinawa, where we would meet up with Ziegfried in just a week. How wonderful that would be. That was the nicest thought, the one I tried to hold on to.

As I crossed over the street, an unusual advertisement in the window of a small corner store caught my eye. A young girl was reaching up to touch the face of an old man, likely her grandfather. There was love in their faces. I stopped. I couldn't help staring at the photo, and my eyes flooded with tears again. Sensei was alone in the dark, in a sunken ship. If he had family somewhere they would never see him again. They would never know what had happened to him. He was spending his last days alone, in solitude and darkness.

In spite of everything Ziegfried had said, in truth, it was *my* decision that Sensei was being abandoned. I was the one who would have to live with that for the rest of my life. Suddenly, without even thinking about it, I turned around and started to walk back the way I had come. I felt a shiver run down my spine, because I knew what I was going to do. I felt like two people now: the one obeying Ziegfried, and the one who wasn't. The second one wasn't thinking about it much, because if I thought about it, I might just end up sitting down on the corner and doing nothing. All I knew was that if I gave up on Sensei, I'd be walking away from everything I believed in. I just couldn't do that.

So I made my way back past Yoshi's house, and on to Hitoshi's house. It was the middle of the night now. The streets were still deserted, and the lights were out in the houses. I went along silently, and never before in my life had I felt so alone. I was coming to a house with an invitation to rob it. How crazy was that? No matter that I was trying to save someone. No matter that I had been given permission in the very oddest way . . . I still had to sneak into someone's house and steal his equipment. The thought of it made my skin crawl.

When I found Hitoshi's house I edged through the gate where we had been before, went past the door and searched for the basement window that Hitoshi had unlocked. Would he have gone to bed by now? I sure hoped so.

There were no lights on. The house, like the city, was as

dark as a tomb. When I found the window, I gave it a gentle push and it opened. I slipped off my sneakers, bent down, and slid my body backwards inside the room. I moved as slowly and silently as I could. I knew Hitoshi meant for me to do this; what else could he have meant? And yet I couldn't help wondering if I had misunderstood. If he woke, I wasn't sure what I would do. Would he come and confront me, or pretend he didn't hear? What if I *had* misunderstood, and he was shocked to see me? What would I do, apologize and try to explain? Try to escape through the window, or make a dash for the door? I didn't know. I just hoped he was a deep sleeper.

The window was high above the floor. It wasn't going to be easy to lift the scuba gear out. Once my feet touched the floor, I crouched down and tried to see everything in the room, but it was too dark. I needed to put the light on. So I gently pushed the door closed and flipped on the light switch. I listened carefully. The loudest sound was the beating of my heart.

On the floor were tanks, hoses, masks, snorkels and fins. There were also other pieces of equipment that I recognized as part of a diver's gear but didn't really know. There seemed to be three sets of everything, so I carefully chose one complete set, with the biggest tank. The smaller pieces I was able to push through the window by standing on my tiptoes, but for the tank I had to move a chair, stand on it, hold the window open with one hand, and slide the tank out. That was really difficult, and made a grating noise. I grimaced and held my breath, waiting and listening for any sound inside the house. There wasn't any. If Hitoshi had heard, he wasn't doing anything about it.

The chair made it a lot easier for me to get back outside. Before I did, I took all the money in my pocket—$200 in American bills—and left it on the floor where the equipment had been. It probably wasn't enough to pay for it, but it was all that I had with me. Then I climbed out the window and shut it, put on my sneakers, picked up the gear, and went out of the yard.

It was heavy. I carried it down the street a ways until I figured out how to fit the tank into the pack and wear it on my back. Now I could walk more quickly, but as it was still heavy and awkward, I had to stop often to rest. Slowly, with many stops, I made my way back to the dockyard.

It was an awfully long way, and I was completely exhausted when I got there. Seaweed was sitting on the hull, and I was so glad to see him. I opened the hatch, greeted Hollie, carried everything inside, and took a long drink of water. I was starving but figured we'd better get out to sea before cooking anything. What if Hitoshi woke, discovered the equipment gone, and called the police so that no one could accuse him of helping me? He probably wouldn't, but I couldn't take that chance. I figured we'd better get out of here just in case.

So I coaxed Seaweed in, shut the hatch, climbed back

down and engaged the batteries. I let water into the tanks and we sank close to the bottom of the marina, just thirty feet deep. But as I was about to put the sub in gear and steer our way out, I pulled the scuba book out of my pocket, where it had been scrunched up all this time, sticking into my belly. As I unfolded it and took a quick peek at the page where it opened, where it showed all the pieces of equipment needed for a dive, I felt confused. I turned and looked at the pieces on the floor. Were they all here? I stared at the book again. There were eight pieces needed. I stared at the floor. I counted seven. That couldn't be. I looked at the book again, and the floor. Maybe two of the pieces were already attached. I checked. No, they weren't. Which was the missing piece? Could I do without it? I sat down, opened the book, and read the page in front of the diagrams. I seemed to be missing the secondary regulator. That's what Sensei would need to breathe through after I rescued him from the ship. I *had* to have it. I couldn't rescue him without it. I dropped my head. I would have to go back and get it.

It was almost five-thirty as I raced down the streets towards Hitoshi's house. I was going as fast as I could, feeling all jittery inside. Was Hitoshi an early riser? Would he be getting up soon? Had he already been up and discovered the robbery? Would there be other people up soon, who might see me sneaking in and out? These questions kept running through my head as I rushed back, filled with anxiety.

How I hated to go back inside the house. Having gotten

away with it once, I didn't feel my chances were as good this time. The sun was coming up soon. People were waking; maybe Hitoshi was, too. I had to get in and out like a shadow.

I made it back to the house half expecting to see the police there, but everything was as it had been before, except I could feel the morning coming. There were lights on in a few of Hitoshi's neighbours' houses, and there was the smell of cooking.

I went through the gate once again, pushed open the window as gently as possible, and listened. It was silent. Well, maybe I could get away with it after all. I squeezed inside the window backwards again, and slid down to the chair that I had left there. I paused and listened. Nothing. Once again I couldn't see anything in the room so I had to turn on the light. As soon as light flooded the room I scanned the floor and saw the other regulator. I couldn't believe I had missed it the first time. The moment I picked it up, I heard a sound in another room. Hitoshi was getting up.

I dashed to the door and flipped off the light. Then I remembered that the door had been open when I had come in the first time, so I very gently pulled it open. This time it creaked a tiny bit. My heart was pounding. I moved to the corner of the door where, if it opened, I could hide. I heard more sounds from the other room. Hitoshi was up, but he was moving slowly. Maybe he didn't know anyone was here. Maybe he was just getting up to pee. Part of me wanted to rush out the window and race down the street.

But I stayed behind the door and waited. It was agonizing. Hitoshi pushed open his bedroom door and walked down the hallway towards the bathroom. I could hear his feet shuffling on the floor, his heavy breathing. He was a large man, and if he were to grab hold of me, I think I'd have a really hard time getting free. But he wouldn't do that, right? I mean, this was his idea, wasn't it?

He shuffled along the floor right past the room where I was. He was moving so slowly I almost thought he had stopped outside the door, but he hadn't. He made his way to the bathroom, and I heard the sounds of him peeing. Should I go now? Or should I wait until he returned to bed? Was he going back to bed, or was he staying up? My heart was beating so fast I wondered if I would have a heart attack.

Hitoshi flushed the toilet, washed his hands, and left the bathroom. But he didn't go back to bed. He went into the kitchen. He was staying up.

I heard the sound of chairs moving in the kitchen, and then the noise of an electric grinder. In a flash I went to the chair, climbed up, and squeezed out the window. But the sound of the grinder ended before I was fully out, and in my rush, the hanging window slipped off my foot and swung back with a bang. *No!* I jumped to my feet and started to run for it.

As I came around to the front of the house, I saw that not only was the kitchen light on, but he had turned on the outside house light too, and the only way I could leave the yard was to pass underneath it. As I did, and as I opened the gate, I turned my head and peered down into the kitchen. There, I saw Hitoshi staring up at me with the strangest look on his face. He didn't look shocked or angry; he just looked sad. He saw me as clearly as could be, and just dropped his eyes with a look of sadness. I didn't know if he was sad because I had taken his equipment, or sad because he had wanted to help me openly, but couldn't. I wasn't about to wait around to find out. I pushed open the gate and ran down the street.

Chapter Eighteen

∽

IT WASN'T DIFFICULT to leave in the early morning. Every available hand must have gone to help areas more badly hit by the tsunami. I waited an hour for a ship to follow out, but when one never came, we just left. We crept along the bottom until we were down to 300 feet, and headed due east. We motored for five hours on battery power, through the blackness, before rising for a peek at the surface and the radar screen. I doubted anyone had seen us or followed us.

On the surface, I opened the hatch to let fresh air pour into the sub and feed the engine. Seaweed went out to ride on the hull. I cranked up the engine to full speed and climbed the portal with Hollie so we could feel the wind in our faces.

It took seventeen hours to return to the spot where we had left Sensei, or where I thought we had left him. I couldn't be absolutely certain it was exactly the same spot, but I knew it was close, or close enough to pick up the dinghy on radar, if it was still around.

Of course it wasn't. It would have drifted. But it also might have sunk, pulled down by the ship. If it had, we'd never find it. We'd be searching for days for nothing.

I shut off the engine and let the sub drift. While it tossed and pitched in choppy waves, I climbed out and threw a buoy into the water to check the current. It appeared to be flowing in the same direction, or nearly the same direction, as when we had left three days earlier. But that was the problem: I couldn't read the flow of the current *exactly*, and even a tiny difference from where we sat could mean a difference of several miles after four days of drifting. We would have to make a wide sweeping search.

Then a new thought occurred to me: what if the ship had sunk just a little deeper, and pulled the dinghy under the surface? I wouldn't be able to see it then, and it wouldn't show up on radar. We might sail right over it without even knowing it.

The hardest thing to do when you are looking for something is to believe that you will find it. If you're looking for someone lost in the woods you can follow a trail, but the sea leaves no trails, and it's very hard not to get discouraged.

I cranked up the engine once again, turned into the current, and sailed a hundred and fifty miles, which took seven and a half hours. And all of that time I scanned the surface with the binoculars, listening for a beep on the radar, yet never saw or heard anything. I turned 90 degrees to starboard, sailed five miles south, and headed back west for fifty miles. That took a little over three hours because of the current and wind. Once again: nothing. It was extremely tiring paying such close attention to the surface.

Another five miles south, I headed east once more for fifty miles. Nothing! Not even a beep on the radar. My heart was heavy, and I was starting to worry about our fuel, but I told myself not to become discouraged. Sensei could not afford for me to give up. Find him!

After two more fifty-mile passes, we had covered a few hundred square miles, and we hadn't found a single thing. Guessing now that the buoy and ship had drifted north of the current, not south, I sailed north twenty-five miles, and began to sweep that area. But it had been two days since I had slept, and I couldn't possibly stay awake anymore. I was so tired, a signal could come and I might not even hear it. So I tossed out the sea anchor, shut the hatch, set my alarm for six hours, and collapsed on my bunk.

It felt like the alarm went off only minutes later, but six hours had passed. I climbed out of bed, put the kettle on, fed the crew, and opened the hatch. It was raining now, and the wind had picked up. The sky was dark and gloomy, and I sensed the current had shifted while I was asleep. I now had a hopeless feeling in my gut. How did you find something out here, where there was only sea and sky, and both were dark, and both were infinitely big?

It seemed to me the current was flowing a little more northerly now, so I tried to account for that as I sailed east once again, turned around, and sailed back five miles north. The sky grew darker, the wind stronger, and the rain fell harder. It wasn't possible to see anything with the binoculars. All we had now was radar and sonar, both of which worked poorly in rough weather. It felt so hopeless.

After two more passes, we were tossing and pitching in high waves, the rain was beating down into the open hatch, and my stomach was growing seasick. It was one thing to sit back and ride through bad weather; it was another to squint through binoculars or stare at electric screens. You might not feel sick on a ride on a roller coaster, but you surely would if you tried to read a book on one. I needed a break.

So I dove to a hundred feet, shut everything off, and lay on my bunk for just a short nap. I never set the alarm because I assumed I'd wake on my own.

Well, I didn't. Exhaustion had caught up to me; it was nine hours later when I woke. I climbed out of bed almost delirious, struggling to remember what I was even doing out here. Then I saw the scuba gear and remembered. If the sea was hiding Sensei and had no intention of releasing him, then maybe he was lost forever. Maybe it *was* hopeless. Maybe Ziegfried had been right all along.

The sea was cruel. I loved it so much, yet I knew it was cruel. It didn't care if you were a good person or a bad person. It didn't care if you were brave or a coward. It didn't care if you were rich or poor, young or old. It didn't care at all. It had just invaded Japan and killed thousands of people, smashing their homes and sweeping them away. And now, perhaps it had decided to take Sensei away, and no matter what I did, it would make no difference. If that's how it was, I would have to accept it—as much as I hated to.

In the end . . . I did. I let go. That was what Ziegfried had ordered me to do. Oddly, it wasn't as hard as I thought it would be. I didn't know if it was my mood, or fatigue, or the knowledge that thousands had died in the tsunami, and many more might die from radiation poisoning; a seed of acceptance settled inside my gut and began to take root. For an hour or so I just puttered around the sub, tidying up, playing with the crew, drinking tea, and wondering if I should try to return Hitoshi's gear. No, I didn't think so. I was sorry I had taken it, but it would be crazy to risk going to prison for that.

After a few hours of resting up, fiddling with my things, and packing the scuba gear away in the cold compartment, I set a course for Okinawa, and tried to get excited about meeting Ziegfried there in less than a week. It would be so wonderful to see him. Would I tell him that I had tried to find Sensei? Perhaps not.

But as we ploughed through the waves heading southwest, I couldn't stop thinking about Sensei. I wondered if he had drowned when seawater found its way into the holds of the ship and pulled her farther down. Had he run out of air first? What a strange and wonderful old man he had been. Perhaps this was the way he would have wanted to go. I didn't know. I didn't like the feeling in my gut, but it had settled there.

I was seasick, too, which didn't happen often, and I was feeling lonely. It was hard not to feel angry at the sea that I loved so much, and hard not to feel like a failure. I had failed to rescue someone when I had been his only hope. I had promised Hollie that we'd find Sensei. I couldn't help feeling he was looking at me now as though I had let him down. But I couldn't turn the ocean inside out by myself! I was just one person; the sea was infinite.

For the longest time I just stood still, with my hand on the periscope shaft, while the sub rode roughly over the choppy waves. I was caught in that unspeakable feeling of wondering what was the meaning of life. What *was* the meaning of life? At that moment I couldn't say. And then, as if someone simply reached over and tapped me gently on the shoulder to answer my question, I heard a small beep come from the sonar screen.

Chapter Nineteen

✧

I CUT THE ENGINE and circled around. Sonar indicated an object twenty feet below us, something small. It could have been garbage, or a sunken container, or even a log. But as I stared at the screen, I saw another object beneath the first one, a much bigger object, sitting at 155 feet. It was over 250 feet long. It had to be the ship. We had found her!

I was over the moon, and yet also gripped by nervousness for the reality of what I was now going to have to do. It made me shiver. She had sunk another twenty feet, and while that didn't seem like much to me, the dive manual said that it was. If you could dive to 130 feet without too much trouble, surely you could dive to 155 feet if you were careful? I mean, how much harder could it be?

I went over a plan in my mind. First I would have to free dive to the dinghy with a rope and tie the sub to it. I didn't like mooring to a sunken ship. What if she suddenly plunged to the bottom? A single rope would snap first; I was certain of that. All the same I chose my thinnest one—strong enough to moor, but not strong enough to pull us under. Then I slipped out of my clothes, took a deep breath, and went over the side.

The sea was dark. I couldn't even see the bright orange dinghy until my head was under water. Then I was spooked because it looked like a whale trying to reach the surface but being held under by a monster. Had the ship pulled the dinghy under gradually, or all of a sudden? I had no idea. All I knew was that if the holds suddenly let water in, or plastic out, she would fall. And if I were tied up in the rope, so would I.

I swam to the dinghy and tied on the rope. Then I swam back, climbed into the sub, pulled all the gear out of the cold room and spread it out on the floor. I sat down with Hollie and Seaweed, opened the manual, and studied how to get started, while my crew pawed and pecked at the hoses that looked like snakes.

Rule number one for beginners: *Never dive alone!* Great.

Rule number two: *breathe continuously*. If you breathe air under pressure, and then hold your breath while you come back up, the air inside of you will expand and burst your lungs. You have to let your breath out on the way up. Okay.

The only problem with that was that I had trained myself to *hold* my breath under water, and that's what kept me alive. Now, I had to go against that natural urge and breathe.

Not only was it important always to breathe, but the slower you breathed, the longer you could stay under water. The manual stressed this over and over. Do everything slowly and calmly. Never get upset. Never over-exert yourself. Never panic. Okay.

Rule number three: *swim like a fish*. Fish are streamlined and move through the water with great efficiency. Try to be like that. You'll save air if you do. Okay.

Rule number four: *maintain neutral buoyancy as much as possible.* You can do that by letting air in and out of the buoyancy compensator—the BC, as they called it—which was part of the backpack, and functioned just like ballast tanks on a sub. You could also drop weights from your belt. But if you did that, and went flying up to the surface in a hurry, you had to remember to keep breathing out, or your lungs would explode. Okay? Okay.

Rule number five: *keep an eye on your air, depth, and time gauges. Know where you are at all times, and how much time (air) you have left.* Okay.

Rule number six: *ascend slowly—no faster than 30 feet a minute, and make a decompression stop at twenty feet below the surface for at least three minutes.* In other words, come back up a lot more slowly than you go down, and stop before you get to the top, otherwise you'll get really sick. Okay.

Rule number seven: *equalize often*. That means clear your ears, either by swallowing or closing your nose and mouth and popping your ears. You have to do this or air can get trapped inside your ear tubes, expand and burst your ear drums, just as you can burst your lungs if you don't breathe out on your way back up. Forgetting to do any of these things can lead to death, and probably will.

Okay. Got it.

The thing I was most concerned about was the diving chart in the book. It showed that the deeper you dived, the less time you could stay down. If you dove the deepest you could safely dive, which in the book was 130 feet, you could only stay for eight minutes. That wasn't much. I had to dive deeper and stay longer.

Before diving to the ship, I planned to make a few practice dives to get comfortable with the equipment. I knew time was precious but I couldn't dive to the ship until I knew I could actually get there.

The first thing to do was fill the tank with air from one of the sub's compressors. That was easy enough and took only five minutes. Then, following the diagrams closely, I fitted all of the pieces of equipment together until the gear looked exactly as it did in the book. I opened the valve on the tank, put the regulator in my mouth, and took a breath. The air flowed almost as easily as regular breathing. That made me feel confident. Then I pulled the gear onto my back like a backpack. But when I tried to stand up from a sitting position it was too heavy. The only way I could get to my feet was to roll to one side, crawl onto my hands and knees, and pull myself up. Then I couldn't squeeze out of the portal with the tank on my back; I had to carry the gear up separately and put it on outside.

Sitting on the hull, with my feet dangling over the water, I went over the rules again and again in my mind as I pulled on the gear, mask, snorkel, and fins. Then I dropped over the side.

Chapter Twenty

⚜

IT WAS STRANGE beyond words to breathe under water, and a good thing I was practising, because the urge to hold my breath was strong, and I had to unlearn it.

I had barely started to look for the dinghy when suddenly it went shooting up over my head. I was sinking too fast! Stay calm I told myself, and let some air into the BC. So I did, and stopped falling. The manual said to try to find perfect buoyancy, using a gentle kick with the fins to go up or down. That was more efficient. So I practised doing that. Only twice did I catch myself holding my breath.

After forty minutes, I returned to the sub, pulled off the

gear, rinsed it off with fresh water, and refilled the tank. Then I fed the crew and lay down for a rest, because the manual said you had to rest between dives or your body couldn't handle the stresses of the pressure. But I couldn't sleep. I was too nervous. I tried to breathe deeply and create a sense of calm in my body—the way Sensei looked when he was meditating on the ship—but my hands and feet kept shaking with the jitters. A few hours later, I climbed out of bed and went for another dive.

This time I went down to sixty feet. I practised reaching behind my head for the spare regulator, the one that Sensei would use. If he didn't have any experience scuba diving I would have to show him what to do while we were under-water, in the dark. The thought that he might panic and burst his lungs, or something else go terribly wrong, worried the heck out of me.

There were a few other problems that I didn't know how to solve. For instance, the ship was sitting at 155 feet, with neutral buoyancy. This must have been because the holds were filled with plastic and air. To get Sensei out of the ship, I had to break into one of them, where he had to be—none of the other rooms on the ship would hold enough air to keep him alive this long. But I had to break into the right one. And once the hold was opened, and water rushed in, that neutral buoyancy would be shattered and the ship would race to the bottom. I would have only seconds to grab him, and Sensei would have to be right at the spot where I broke in.

Then there was *nitrogen narcosis*. This was when nitrogen in the pressurized air prevented oxygen from getting to your brain, so you suffered a loss of judgement, loss of motor skills, dizziness, confusion, and euphoria. It could happen as soon as you reached 100 feet, but was different for everybody. You could avoid it longer, and handle it better, if you stayed calm and breathed slowly. Seemed to me that that was the answer to everything—staying calm.

Back in the sub I filled the tank for the third and hopefully last time. But now a completely different worry occurred to me: what would happen to my crew if I didn't make it back? That was a troubling thought.

And so, although it made me very sad, and though I was trying to stay in a positive mood, I sat down and wrote a letter, then taped it to the control panel. The letter read:

To Whoever finds this letter:

This is my dog. His name is Hollie. If I am not here, it is because I didn't make it back up from trying to rescue a man who is trapped in a ship below us. Hollie is a very good dog. Please take good care of him, and please find a good home for him. I found him on the sea, and he loves being near water. His favourite thing is running on the beach. If you see a seagull nearby, he is part of my crew too. His name is Seaweed. He is very smart. Seaweed and Hollie are like brothers, and I hope you can keep Seaweed too. If you can't, I know he will survive anyway because he

is incredibly resourceful. But please let him stay on your
ship until you are close enough to land to let him fly there.
If you find this letter and I am not here, please call the
number below and tell them what happened. Thank you.

Alfred Pynsent

I carried out all the dog food I had, and all the bread,
cookies, and other things that Hollie and Seaweed would
eat, and left it in such a way that they could get into it if they
were hungry enough. Then I filled all the pots I had with
fresh water, and left the tap of the fresh water tank dripping
slowly into a pot. I figured they would probably survive a
few weeks if nobody came before then. Although I would
leave the hatch open, I would tie a burlap sack across it to
keep them from climbing out. It would be okay if Seaweed
escaped, but not Hollie. I carried all of the gear up, including my flashlight and a heavy wrench. I tied the wrench to
my belt. I would use it to bang on the hull of the ship.

I pulled on all the gear, called down to Hollie and Seaweed
that I'd be back, took a deep breath, and went over the side.

Like a fish I swam straight down, keeping my hands at my
sides, and propelling myself with slow easy fin kicks. I tried
to imagine I was a snowflake falling into a silent forest, except
for the sound of my breathing. As I approached the dinghy I
veered slightly away from it, went around it, and kept falling.

Down, down I drifted into increasing darkness. Ever so
gradually the pressure began to squeeze me. I shut my nose

and mouth and cleared my ears. At seventy-five feet the pressure was something I was familiar with. Yet because I was not holding my breath as I was used to and was wearing all this gear, it felt unnatural. In fact, as I approached 100 feet, I began to struggle with a feeling of claustrophobia for the first time in my life. I wished I wasn't wearing any gear at all, and just holding my breath. I wanted to unstrap myself from the pack. When I hit 130 feet, I was shocked at the intensity of the pressure and was fighting back feelings of panic.

I looked down through the darkness at the ship's hull and saw gloomy shadows of weeds and sea growth rising from her keel. Panic filled my chest. I couldn't seem to get a grip on it. The ship looked as though she were just waiting to grab me and pull me down to the bottom. I glanced at the depth gauge but it was blurry. I glanced at the air gauge but the needle was swinging back and forth. Was I out of air? Suddenly my ears began to ache very sharply. I cleared them, and then, without thinking, turned around and headed back towards the safety of the surface.

It was a long ascent. I stopped at 20 feet and waited for a few minutes. I was terribly disappointed in myself. It would be hours before I could try again.

Back on the sub I felt a little sick so I lay down in bed. The walls were spinning. I wanted to go over the events of the dive carefully but could hardly concentrate. The manual said to rest, but how could you rest when you were filled with anxiety? For hours I tossed and turned on the cot, trying to meditate, trying to relax, but couldn't seem to do either. What was Sensei doing right now? What was he thinking? Did he think I had given up? Hang on, Sensei, I kept saying to myself over and over. Just hang on.

∽

I didn't remember falling asleep, but a few hours later I woke to a tossing and pitching sub, and a terrible feeling of urgency. How much air did Sensei have left? Why was I wasting time? Why hadn't I rescued him already? Was I just going to find a corpse?

Hollie came over and jumped onto my lap. I scratched his ears and patted his head. What a loyal dog he was. What a wonderful and true friend. Remembering how Sensei had played with him on the ship, I wished we could be back there now, on the hot sunny deck, eating fresh tomatoes and garlic, and feeling the warm Pacific breeze on our skin. "Rescue him," I whispered to myself. "Rescue him. He doesn't deserve to die like this."

Feeling much less confident than before, I rose to my feet and wandered over to the control panel. There I saw something that made my heart shudder. The ship had dropped another 17 feet, breaking the rope and pulling the dinghy under once again. The ship was now sitting at 172 feet below the surface. It must have just happened; otherwise we would have drifted farther away than we had. Before I could dive to the ship I would have to find the dinghy rope first, and retie it to the sub.

Shaking with nervousness, I fed the crew and made a breakfast that I could barely eat. I went outside and made a quick free dive down to the dinghy, found the rope, and tied it to a rope from the sub. Then I climbed back inside and prepared for the dive that I knew had to succeed.

My hands kept shaking as I filled the tank and carried the gear outside. I couldn't seem to calm myself. The sky was darker now, and the sub was tossing around. That made no difference below but I sure hoped a storm wasn't coming.

I breathed deeply, closed my eyes, and told myself that everything was going to be okay. This dive wasn't about me; it was about Sensei. I went over the rules again and again, and told myself it was all right to have claustrophobic feelings, and that I could do this. "Just don't give up," I said out loud, and went over the side.

Chapter Twenty-one

✌

AS I DRIFTED DOWN into the darkness I broke another rule in the manual: I filled the BC with water and let my weight and the weight of the wrench and gear pull me down fast. It only made sense to me to fall quickly and save energy and air by not using my legs. After all, the manual warned only about rising too fast, not about descending. I could refill the BC with air once I was down there, and restore neutral buoyancy. This was not a pleasure dive; this was a rescue mission. It had been seven days since the ship went down. I couldn't afford to waste any more time.

I had to assume that Sensei didn't have any experience

with scuba diving, and I would have to try to explain with gestures how he must keep breathing and clearing his ears. The best way, I figured, was to demonstrate it. But it would be dark down there, and I'd have to shine the flashlight on me when I did.

The bigger problem was how to get him out of the ship without drowning him when the water rushed in. It wouldn't pour in, as it would near the surface; it would *explode* in. By banging on the hull with the wrench, I was hoping to lead him to a door or a hatch, wait for him to open it, and grab him. It seemed impossibly risky but what other options were there?

Falling with negative buoyancy turned out to be a good thing. I fell at a steady pace that was maybe a little too fast, but I didn't have to kick at all or steer with my legs. I used less air, and when the pressure began to squeeze, I stayed calmer than before. At 120 feet the gauges were still clear. Although I was beginning to feel uncomfortable, I was not panicking.

At 150 feet the gauges were blurry again, and I was beginning to feel confused. Long fat ribbons of seaweed rose up from the bottom of the ship, and I had to squeeze between them. I felt as though I were falling into a dark abyss. I tried counting to ten to calm my fears. It helped. A few seconds later, my hand came in contact with the keel.

I felt dizzy when I touched the ship, as if I had touched an electric wire. I was confused. I swam around the keel and down along the crusted hull until the pressure was so intense my face felt as if it were in a can opener. The hull was endless, but once I rounded the ship's belly, I let air into the BC and stopped falling. It was hard to do. I couldn't seem to concentrate very well. Even turning the air valve was almost too difficult. I pointed my flashlight. The deck's railing was just below. I glanced at the gauges, but they were too fuzzy to read. How deep was I now? I didn't know. How much air did I have? I didn't know. My ears were aching badly, so I cleared them, but they still ached. What was I doing here? I felt completely confused. And then, something altogether different began to happen.

For the life of me I couldn't explain it, but suddenly everything just got a whole lot easier. Even with all the incredible pressure squeezing against me, I began to feel as light as a feather. This wasn't so difficult after all. This was fun. I couldn't even remember what all the fuss had been about. And then I realized . . . this wasn't just any old ship . . . this was the *Titanic*!

Though I knew the *Titanic* had gone down in the Atlantic, not the Pacific, here she was next to me! She must have drifted here. How remarkable that I had found her. Wow! I couldn't wait to tell Ziegfried and Sheba. I wondered if there was a telephone down here that I could use. I decided to look for one.

But I had to find Sensei, too, so I decided to do both. I pulled the wrench from my belt and hammered it against the hull. *Bang, bang, bang!* I listened for a response but there wasn't one. Where was Sensei? Was he sleeping? I'd better wake him up. *Bang, bang, bang, bang, bang, bang, bang . . .* "Wake up, Sensei!" I said. My ears ached. "Oh, buggers!" I said, and cleared them. What a nuisance. You try to wake somebody up to borrow their telephone and all your ears can do is ache.

It occurred to me that maybe I wasn't banging the right tune. Maybe Sensei would wake up only if I banged the right tune on the hull. So I started to bang the rhythm of "Frère Jacques." But that was pretty boring, and I never got a response. This was a pretty boring place down here, all things considered. Where was Sensei? What a sleepyhead. My ears ached again, so I cleared them again. Then I remembered I'd better breathe slowly. "Breathe slow," I said to myself. Then I sang it. "*Breathe slow . . . sweet chariot . . . coming for to carry me home. Breathe slow, sweet chariot, coming for to carry me home.*"

This was a song my grandmother used to sing. Sensei would surely love this song, I thought, as I pulled myself around the railing and underneath the deck and over to the doorway where Sensei liked to do his one-legged squats. It was completely dark, so I didn't think he would be doing his exercises now. He only liked to do them in the daytime. I shone my flashlight on the door. It was open, so I swam inside.

"*If you get to Heaven before I do . . . comin' for to carry me home . . . Breathe slow, sweet chariot . . . comin' for to carry me home.*" I wasn't sure those were the right words, but I sang them the way my grandmother did on her rocking chair back home, and I banged on the top of the aft hold, and the sound echoed inside. That meant it was hollow, like an empty coconut. No one answered, so I swam to the entrance to the mid-hold, and banged on it. I got only a dull sound there, so I knew that hold was full, just like in the story of *The Three Bears*: Mama Bear's bowl was cold.

So I swam to the third hold, the fore hold, and banged on it with the wrench. The sound echoed. This one was empty. Then . . . I heard someone banging back. That was funny. There was somebody inside. Hmmm. I was getting dizzy, but I was so happy. Why was there somebody inside the *Titanic*? Had they been here all this time? Wow. They probably had a really long beard. That would be an interesting story in the newspaper. I should tell somebody.

I banged on the door of the hold again. *Bang, bang, bang!*

Bang, bang, bang! came the answer. Hmmm! That was interesting. They were mimicking me. I did it again, just one bang. And so did they. I banged twice. They banged twice. Funny! So I banged fourteen times, and they banged back exactly fourteen times. Okay. They win. For a prize, I will let them out.

I swam to the door, and banged on it twice. *Knock, knock!* Anybody home? Do you want to come out? The person inside knocked back once. I thought that meant yes, they were ready to come out. Okay, I said. I'm ready. But my ears ached a heck of a lot. I cleared them, but couldn't stop them from aching. What a nuisance! What a boring place! Come on outside and let's go somewhere else that's more interesting. Who would ever have known that the *Titanic* was such a boring place?

And then the door opened a crack, and a metal hook shot out and grabbed the doorjamb. Then a skinny arm reached out and grabbed my arm, and squeezed me tighter than all the pressure of the water. But I was so dizzy I wasn't really sure what was happening. I steadied my flashlight. Hey, there's Sensei! He looks different down here in the darkness. He is so small, and his hair is so white, and the look on his face is scary. Then the door burst open, and the dark sea poured into it. I felt it tug at me, too, but Sensei was wearing some sort of metal harness, like a ladder, that allowed him to crawl out against the water rushing in, and he held onto me and dragged me through the passageway, and out a doorway to the deck. Suddenly the *Titanic* started to yell and scream. She didn't like us banging on her doors. I didn't know why she was so angry but it was awful. I didn't want to stay here and listen to that. "Hey, Sensei," I said, "I don't want to listen to that, do you?"

But he didn't answer. He slipped out of his metal harness and kept pulling me sideways as the *Titanic* started to fall below us. It banged into us and tried to take us with it, but Sensei shook his head and pointed up. He wanted to go to the surface. Okay, I thought. That's a good idea. I nodded my head. "Maybe you would like this," I said, and reached behind my head for the second regulator. I handed it to him, and then made the gesture of breathing that I had practised. Sensei took the regulator and put it in his mouth, and together we started swimming up.

But now I was so very dizzy, confused, and seasick that I just wanted to lie down on my bed. It was such a long way up, and I didn't feel like making the trip. Something told me we weren't supposed to go up so fast, but Sensei seemed to be in an awful hurry. "Slow down!" I tried to say, but he wouldn't listen to me. "We have to stop!" I said. I was still dizzy, but I was starting to remember where we were. "We must slow down!" I said, and I tried to gesture to him. I looked at the gauges. We had risen to 100 feet. The ship was falling below us, and large bubbles were racing past us on their way to the surface. The ship was making terrible screams. "Just go!" I yelled at the ship. If ever a ship deserved to go to the bottom, it was this one. I didn't even feel sorry for her anymore; I just wanted her to sink.

At seventy-five feet my head was much clearer but I felt terribly sick. I could see Sensei's face better now without the flashlight. He looked sick, too. He wasn't swimming anymore. He looked like he wanted to go to sleep too. *Breathe!* I took the regulator out of my mouth and blew bubbles and gestured to him with my hand. He nodded his head but he was sleepy now. I pushed my hand against his stomach and said, "*Breathe!*"

At fifty feet, Sensei wasn't communicating with me any-more, and I was feeling terribly sick. I was afraid I was going to throw up into the regulator. It was getting harder to breathe. I looked at the gauges. No wonder. There was no air left.

Chapter Twenty-two

⌒

I BROKE THE SURFACE and saw Seaweed squawking on the hatch. He had squeezed past the burlap sack. I could hardly hear him. My head was splitting, and I was sick to my stomach. When I looked for Sensei, I saw him bobbing slowly to the surface, but he wasn't moving on his own. Only now did I see that he was wearing a strap with metal bottles around his waist. This was helping him float. On his back was strapped the long bamboo sheath that held his sword.

For a second I feared he was dead but he choked and coughed up seawater. Then I knew that he was alive, although unconscious. I unhooked the scuba tank, slipped out of the gear, and let it fall. I couldn't help Sensei when I was wrapped up in it, especially with the way I was feeling. I could barely stay afloat myself.

I took hold of Sensei under his arms and pulled him to the sub. He was thinner than before, and probably hadn't eaten for eight days. When your body has no fat to burn, it will eat its own muscle.

We leaned against the railing and rested. A little blood was coming from one of his ears. He had burst his eardrum. I put my fingers to my ears, and one of them was bleeding also. That's why I couldn't hear Seaweed. This was the second time in my life I had burst an eardrum. It would take months to heal properly. But we were alive, and Sensei was no longer trapped down in the ship. I couldn't quite believe it.

But was he okay? He was breathing but didn't look good.

It was hard to get him up the ladder and into the sub. I thought I was going to faint and drop him. He did slip the last few feet inside the portal because it was impossible to hold him and squeeze down the ladder at the same time. He landed on the wooden floor with a bump that seemed to wake him for a second or two. Then he rolled over and went back to sleep. Hollie came over and started licking his face but Sensei didn't respond. I pulled out my camping mat and pillow, rolled Sensei onto it, then dropped onto my bed with a bucket and threw up.

The walls were spinning like a merry-go-round, my head was throbbing with pain, and my stomach was the sickest it had ever been. There was nothing I could do to feel better but fall asleep, which took a long time. I just lay in my bed and watched the walls spin and spin, and felt the sickness in my stomach that I kept asking to go away but wouldn't.

When I woke, the walls were still spinning, and my headache was severe. I was still stomach sick but not as badly as before. It hurt to raise my head, but I wanted to check on Sensei. He had moved. He was lying next to Hollie beside the observation window with his eyes open but glassy.

I sat up, dangled my feet over my cot, and waited to feel better before standing up. It never happened, so I got up anyway, made my way to the stove and put on the kettle. I looked at Sensei. He was staring at Hollie, who was staring back at him sympathetically. Hollie was the most sympathetic dog in the world. He knew when you weren't feeling well, and would do everything he could to make you feel better.

When the tea was ready, I poured two cups, put powdered milk and sugar in them, and carried them over to the observation window, spilling them because my hands were shaking so badly. Hollie's tail was wagging. I sat down beside Sensei and offered him a cup. His eyes were droopy. He was feeling horrible, too. He nodded his head a little but didn't reach for the cup. So I put it down beside him. Hollie stuck his nose in it. "Not for you, Hollie," I said. My voice sounded far away. I raised my cup and took a sip. The tea was wonderful in my throat. It was a miracle we were alive.

After a while I began to feel a little better. I made a pot of porridge and ate it with lots of brown sugar. I couldn't get Sensei to take a bite, and he still hadn't touched his tea. I bent down next to him and looked into his eyes. "Are you okay?" I asked. I made a thumbs-up sign and questioned him with my eyes. He tossed his head a little, and raised his thumb. At least he could hear me. Then he curled up in a ball and went back to sleep. He didn't use the mat or pillow. I brought them over but he just shut his eyes. "Okay," I said. "Sleep. I'll make you some fresh tea when you wake."

We were at least three or four days' sail from Okinawa, where Ziegfried was probably already waiting, which meant that we were three or four days late. I knew that Ziegfried would wait at least a week, if not more, but he would be worried. I felt badly about that.

But the feeling was nothing compared to the fact that I had disobeyed him. How was I going to explain that?

There was no point in worrying about it now. I just had to get us there. So I sealed the hatch, submerged to a hundred feet, where the sea was peaceful, engaged the batteries and pointed us in the direction of Okinawa.

Sensei's decompression sickness was worse than mine, not because he was older, I thought, but because he hadn't breathed enough on the way up. He had burst an eardrum, but his lungs seemed to be okay. There was no blood coming from his mouth, and he wasn't struggling to breathe. I did finally manage to have him drink a little tea. I carried over a fresh cup when I saw him stirring after another sleep. We had been quietly cutting through the water at sixteen knots for a few hours, but now we had to surface to recharge the batteries.

Once he finished the tea, I rose to the surface, opened the hatch, and turned on the engine. A light rain fell down through the portal, collected in the trough below the floor, to be removed later by the sump pumps. I watched Sensei stare at the rain as if it were a miracle. In the belly of the ship he must have believed he was going to die.

As the sub ploughed through choppy waves in darkness and rain, I stood at the stove and cut vegetables for a stew. I fried onions in oil, and sprinkled them with salt, pepper, and spices. Though I could barely hear the onions sizzle, the smell rose out of the pot, and Sensei turned his head towards it. A small smile appeared on his face. He must have been starving.

Once the stew was ready, I carried him a bowl. But his hand was so shaky he could hardly hold the spoon. The stew kept falling off and Hollie kept licking it up. From a whole bowl of stew he had maybe a third. But he had bread, too, and chewed it very slowly, as if he were falling asleep. He never rose to his feet. I showed him where the bucket was for using the toilet, but he just nodded weakly. He was so sick. So I brought the bucket over and put it down beside him. Then he closed his eyes and slept for another ten hours.

When he finally woke, he seemed a little better. He wanted

to know where we were going. I carried over a map, pointed to where we were, then pointed to where we were headed.

"*Okinawa!*" he said. He put his hand on his heart and shut his eyes. When he opened them, they were wet with tears.

Chapter Twenty-three

❧

THE MAN LYING on the floor was not the man I had known on the ship. Seven days without food or light, without good water, and certainly without fresh air, had seemed to shrink him to half the size he had been, which wasn't very big to start. On top of that he had been injured on the way to the surface. How injured I didn't know, but he needed medical attention. His breathing seemed shallower all the time, though I couldn't hear well enough really to tell.

One unexpected effect of his condition was that he began to talk. He struggled at first, speaking very slowly, stopping often to rest. Yet he seemed driven to do it, as if he felt he had to explain himself—not to me in particular, just to somebody. I was an eager listener. Like everything else about him his thoughts were well organized and came out clearly, as if he had been practising them the whole time he had been trapped in the ship.

"My father was a strict man. I never saw him smile, ever . . . He was a traditionalist. Everything about old Japan he loved . . . With me, he was very strict, very hard. He told me what I would do, what I would think, what my life would be like from start to finish . . . But I rebelled. Like you, I wanted to see the world. I wanted to be free . . . My father tried to change me. He gave me many beatings before I ran away."

Sensei spoke softly. I had to sit right beside him to hear him above the ringing in my head. I didn't want to miss a word.

"My father was a very strong man. Me, I was just a skinny boy . . . Sixteen or seventeen. On my last beating, my father broke my arm . . . He had been teaching me ninjutsu, and was frustrated with me. I was too slow, too lazy. The next day, I left in the middle of the night . . . I never saw him again. Many years later I came back to see my mother. My father was dead then . . . I stood at his grave, and wept."

Sensei paused to rest and catch his breath.

"Were you born in Okinawa?"

"Yes. But I left to travel the world. I worked on ships. I did everything: cooking, cleaning, loading, unloading . . . I

worked every day. I learned many skills. When I wasn't work-
ing, I would read . . . I travelled to America, to Europe, to
Canada, to Australia. I have been to Montreal many times."
He smiled.

"I taught myself English by reading English books. Mark
Twain. Jack London. Joseph Conrad. Charles Dickens . . . "

Sensei winced and held his head with his hand.

"Are you okay?"

He looked wearily into my eyes. "I am still alive. That is
not so bad. I thought I would die with my ship, but you are
very determined . . . You do not '*give up*.'" He smiled again.
"I think you and I are not so different."

I shrugged. "You would have done the same for me."

"I would."

"Where did you get your ship?"

"My ship." Sensei dropped his head and swung it side to
side. "My ship has been with me for a long time. So many
times I thought I was losing her, but she has always stayed
with me. Now, finally, she is gone. All things pass away, even
us."

"I am sorry."

He shook his head and took a sip of tea. I was anxious for
him to continue.

"When did you get your ship?"

"After the war."

"The Second World War?"

"Yes. I returned to Japan and served in the navy. Three

times I was wounded from explosions on our ship . . . Not from the enemy. We carried weapons to the islands. It was very dangerous. So many people died. Young men like you. Then the bombs . . . and then it was over." He took another drink of tea.

"And then?"

"After the war, ships were very cheap. I had saved all my money. I had American money. Very good in Japan then."

"So you bought your own ship?"

He nodded. "I bought my ship, hired a crew, and began to transport plastic."

"Plastic?" I was surprised.

"For many years I carried plastic goods around the world. Japanese industry grew very quickly after the war. Every-where was plastic now. Everyone wanted it. Everyone liked it . . . It was new. It was cheap. What we used to make with ivory, shell, glass, and wood, we now made with plastic. It was easy to pack and transport. It didn't break. You couldn't destroy it . . . I made lots of money. I never thought about the environment. I never thought about the sea . . . Every day, every week, every month, every year, we filled my ship with all things plastic and carried them around the world. I believed we were doing good service to humanity."

Sensei laughed, and then coughed. It didn't sound good.

"When did it change for you? When did you start to feel differently?"

"Not for a very long time. First, I bought a plastics factory."

"You owned a plastics factory?" I couldn't believe it. "Did you stop sailing?"

"For a while. I got married. I settled down."

"Did you have children?"

"No. My wife could not have children."

He paused. He was far away in his memory.

"She was sick for a long time. It was cancer. When she died, they told me she had been poisoned by my factory. Everyone got sick. Even I was sick too, but not with cancer. We didn't know then how harmful the chemicals were when the plastic was hot. We didn't wear masks . . . "

"I'm sorry to hear about your wife."

"A long time ago. Then, I went back to sea. I became healthy again. I began to practise the ninjutsu my father had forced me to learn when I was young . . . All of the things he had taught me came back to me. It felt like he was there with me again. I wished I had been a better student. I wished I had been a better son. And then . . . "

"And then?"

"I began to see garbage in the sea. Every day more garbage than the day before. It was as if the land had become full, and it was now spilling over into the sea."

"Plastic?"

"Yes, plastic, and nets, and dead animals. One day I saw a dolphin struggling with a plastic ring around its neck. I tried to save it but I was too late. It strangled itself to death."

"I've seen things like that, too."

"Yes. But this plastic ring had my name on it. It was made in my factory."

"Oh."

Sensei took a drink of tea and spoke over the cup. I had to lean closer to hear him.

"It took me forty-five years to learn that everything I was doing was wrong. I was getting rich but I was destroying life. What good is that, to have money, but kill the very life that we love, kill the people we love, kill the sea? This is crazy. We humans are crazy."

"I know."

"So I closed my factory. I shut it down. I left everything behind and went to sea in my old ship, alone. I began to pick up plastic from the sea. I could never pick up a fraction of what I had manufactured but I could start . . . A journey of a thousand miles starts with one step . . . At seventy-five years of age I began to really live for the first time. I came to understand that we humans are just like the dolphins. No more important, no less. Now, I live for life, for the sea, for my garden."

"I'm sorry you lost your garden. It was so wonderful."

Sensei put his hand to his chest. "My garden is here. I carry it with me always."

I nodded.

"Many times I have sailed my ship full of plastic to recycling plants in Tokyo. They think I am crazy there. I tell them we are all crazy, but it is better to save life than destroy it."

"What will you do now?"

"Now, I will visit my brother in Okinawa. He has children. His children have children. He has always asked me to visit him. Now I think I will."

"Is he as old as you?"

"No. He is younger. He is just a young man, maybe only ninety-two." Sensei laughed a little, and then was overcome with coughing. A little blood came up when he did.

Chapter Twenty-four

∽

TWO DAYS LATER, as we approached Okinawa, Sensei's condition worsened dramatically. He had stopped talking the day before. He seemed to go in and out of sleep, but his sleep was not restful. His breathing was so laboured, I was beginning to believe that his lungs had been damaged after all. With my help, I could get him to drink tea, but no longer to eat. I needed to get him to a hospital as quickly as possible. He was wasting away.

When I spied the north of the island with the binoculars I felt hopeful, but by then Sensei had slipped into unconsciousness and I was also beginning to feel desperate. It was the middle of the night. I motored up and down the north of the island, looking for a fire on the beach but not finding one. When I was pretty sure I had found the most northerly of the beaches, I dropped anchor, inflated the dinghy, and rowed to the beach.

It was a starry night and the moon was still out. I could see the silhouettes of logs and rocks on the beach but no tents. Had Ziegfried already come and gone?

Hollie charged out of the dinghy like a cannonball. Then he began to scour every inch of sand and rock as fast as he could. Nobody ever loved a beach as much as he did, not even Seaweed, who was already here, attacking scurrying crabs in the moonlight.

I pulled the dinghy above the high tide line and tied it to the heaviest log I could find, though it wasn't windy. With poor hearing it was harder to gauge the elements.

I was nervous. How was I going to explain to Ziegfried what had happened? Would he be angry? Would he be disappointed in me? That's what worried me the most. But I just couldn't have lived with myself if I had let Sensei die. Would Ziegfried understand that? I was so nervous about it, I was jittery.

Where was he? I walked up and down the beach looking for a tent, or a car, or a campfire, or extra-large footsteps, or any evidence he had been here, and found nothing. The horizon was blue now. The sun was coming up. Where was Hollie? He was here a few minutes ago. It was confusing when you couldn't hear properly, and your head was ringing constantly. I was so tired. I just wanted to go to bed and wake up to find everything was better. And then I felt a heavy hand come down on my shoulder. I nearly jumped out of my sneakers. I turned around, and there was Ziegfried, with a confused look on his face.

He called my name, but the ringing inside my head was so loud now I could barely hear him. He reached over and gave me one of his great bear hugs, which prevented me from breathing until he let go, which took a while. When he did, I almost fell. Ziegfried was speaking quickly, with excited gestures, but I wasn't following him. He looked confused. What was wrong? He questioned me with his face. I pointed to my ear and shook my head. And then, try as I might, I couldn't keep my tears from falling.

Ziegfried dropped his hand sympathetically onto my shoulder, gesturing for me to sit down on the sand, which I did. He did too, and Hollie jumped all over him. Seaweed landed beside us and just stared. Ziegfried reached over and gently touched my ear, which made me pull away. He said one word, slowly and clearly. "How?"

I dropped my head. I felt ashamed. When I raised it, I saw a deeply sympathetic look on his face.

"Did you rescue the old man?"

I nodded my head.

"Is he alive?"

I nodded again. "Yes, but he's really sick."

"He's in the sub?"

"Yes."

Ziegfried raised his eyebrows in disbelief. He didn't seem angry. "Where?"

"Out there." I pointed out to where the sub was sitting in the water. You couldn't see it from the beach.

"And the sub? She's okay?"

"Yes, but we've got to get Sensei to the hospital right away."

"Okay, Al. Bring the sub in as close as you can. I'll help you get the old man into the dinghy, and we'll take him to the hospital in Naha. Okay?"

"Okay."

We jumped up, put the dinghy back in the water, and I paddled out, climbed in, and brought the sub as close to the beach as possible. Ziegfried walked out to his chest, climbed onto the hull, reached down into the portal, and took hold of Sensei as I pushed him up from below. Sensei was non-responsive. I was really afraid for him now.

"He doesn't look good, Al. I'll take him to the beach and put him in the car. After you go and hide the sub as best you can, I'll come back out in the dinghy to get you."

"Okay."

I did as I was told. I tied the sub between rocks off shore. It worried me the hull would scrape against the rocks if the weather turned foul but there was nowhere else to moor it.

I let enough water into the tanks to sink the hatch an inch below the surface. Water rushed in before I could climb out and seal the hatch, but the sump pumps would remove it. The sub could be spotted from the air only if someone was looking for it but was invisible from the beach and water.

Once Ziegfried appeared in the dinghy, we made our way to his rented car, where Sensei was lying unconscious in the backseat. Hollie climbed onto my lap in the front, and Seaweed rode on the roof as we pulled onto the road. The car leaned close to the road on Ziegfried's side. We both felt very tense because we didn't know if Sensei was going to make it, although we didn't talk about that.

"Sheba sends her love, Al."

I had to look at Ziegfried to hear him. The ringing in my head was loud and distracting.

"How was your trip?"

"Not too bad. I was alone on the plane. No one wants to travel to Japan right now. This nuclear meltdown is a big deal, Al. Nobody knows how bad it will be, except that it's really bad."

"Thousands died in the tsunami."

"I know. We saw it on TV. A natural disaster and then a man-made one, all at the same time." Ziegfried shook his head. "What a catastrophe."

"Have you been here long?"

"A few days. I thought about renting a boat and boathouse already, but didn't want to leave the area in case you arrived. I've rented a cabin in a little town called Kunigami, but we've got to go straight to Naha now, to the hospital. How's he doing, Al? Is he breathing?"

I turned around and put my hand on Sensei's chest. "Yes, he's breathing."

"Check his pulse, Al."

I reached back again, took Sensei's wrist, and felt for his pulse.

"Here. Take my watch. Count how many beats you feel in a minute, okay?"

"Okay."

Sensei's pulse was weak and slow. I didn't like the feel of it. "Thirty-seven."

"Thirty-seven? Are you sure? You'd better count it again, Al."

"Okay." So I did. "Thirty-nine."

"That's pretty slow. Keep checking his breathing. We've got three hours to the hospital, I think."

We drove along the small road through a rocky, tropical landscape that reminded me of Saipan. Ziegfried's side of the car leaned so close to the road that it scraped a few times. I settled into my seat, with Hollie on my lap, and kept an eye on Sensei.

Although I had slept the night before, and the night before that, I couldn't seem to stay awake. It was so much warmer on land than at sea, and the movement of the car, so smooth and steady, kept lulling me to sleep. I tried hard to stay awake to listen to Ziegfried, but my head kept falling forward. It was such a long drive to the hospital that I was asleep long before we got there.

Ziegfried carefully opened the door and helped me out.

He had already taken Sensei into the emergency ward. Now he had a worried look on his face for me. Was there anything *else* wrong with me, he wanted to know? I didn't think so. Decompression sickness and a burst eardrum were enough, weren't they? Ziegfried frowned as he stared at my sweaty head. No. There must be something else.

As usual, he was right.

Chapter Twenty-five

❦

SENSEI HAD A collapsed lung. He had picked up an infection that turned into pneumonia and collapsed the lung. The doctor told us that if we hadn't brought him in when we did, it was unlikely he would have survived another night. Did he have family nearby? Yes, I said, he had a brother and other family, but I didn't know who or where they were. What was his name? I didn't know that either. I only knew him as Sensei. I knew that he was born on Okinawa, and that he was one hundred years old.

"Many people in Okinawa are very old," said the doctor. "Other than this issue, he appears to be extremely healthy for his age. He is, however, severely dehydrated."

"He was trapped in a ship under the sea for seven days," I said.

The doctor stared at us wide-eyed. "He was caught in the tsunami?"

"Yes. I think one of his eardrums is burst too."

The doctor wrote these things in his chart. "We will take care of him. When he is conscious, we will find out who he is, and contact his family. Please keep checking in with us so we can let you know how he is doing."

"Okay. Thank you."

Ziegfried and I shook hands with the doctor and left the hospital.

Next we went to a medical clinic, where a doctor looked into my ears, which was very painful, and prescribed the same medication I had taken back in India, where I first burst my eardrums. Don't do it again, the doctor warned, or you will likely damage your hearing permanently. Will they heal completely, I asked? Possibly, the doctor said, but it will take a while. You can expect to feel weak and dizzy for a few more days.

After my ears, the doctor examined my lymph nodes, looked into my eyes, listened to my heart and lungs, and had a nurse take my blood. This was at Ziegfried's urging. He was concerned that I had been exposed to radiation in Choshi. I was lethargic and listless, Ziegfried told them. I thought I was just tired. But when the blood test was analyzed the next day, it showed that my iron and vitamin B12 were very low. I wasn't eating enough red meat, the doctor concluded. That was true enough; I wasn't eating any. Low iron and low B12 would make me tired all the time, the doctor said. Eat red meat. I shook my head.

"He is a stubborn young man," the doctor said to Ziegfried.

Ziegfried frowned. "You have no idea."

When we left the clinic for the second time, we went in search of foods with lots of iron and B12. We bought nuts, seeds, raisins, grains, broccoli, spinach, blackstrap molasses, and nutritional yeast. Plenty of iron and B12 in those foods, Ziegfried assured me. That worked for me. Why kill animals if we don't have to?

Next, we had to find a place to refit the sub. I thought she was fit enough for the return trip to Newfoundland, but Ziegfried shook his head. "Not a chance."

He wanted to overhaul the engine, clean out all the pipes, clean and re-test the valves, replace electrical wires and fuses, test the propeller and crank shaft for metal fatigue, test the fittings around the hatch and observation window, and scrape and repaint the hull.

"That would take six months!" I said.

"We've got three weeks," he answered. "We'll work flat out." But first he would make a close overall inspection.

So we went back to the north of the island. I brought the sub closer to the beach, where Ziegfried could walk out to her and climb inside. He looked like a bear trying to squeeze into a rabbit hole. I stayed on the beach and played with Hollie, made a campfire, and roasted potatoes and vegetables in tin foil. Ziegfried spent about two hours inside the sub, which must have given him a stiff neck, because he couldn't even stand up. When he came out and returned to the beach, he had a severe look on his face. That worried me, but his findings weren't as bad as they could have been.

"She's not too bad, really" he said, wiping grease off his hands with sand and water. "The engine's running well, but needs a cleaning. She could use new valves pretty much everywhere, in the compressors, air exchangers, gauges, tanks. Batteries need topping up. You're not getting full electrical power."

I nodded. He was incredibly strict about these things.

"She's running well, but she's tired, like you. Not burning air and fuel as well as she ought to. I need to see the hull better. Let's eat, and then I'll borrow your goggles."

I didn't think my mask would fit Ziegfried at all and was surprised he would plan to go underneath the sub because he had such a fear of drowning. That showed just how dedicated he was.

But first we sat on the sand and had a feed. I told Ziegfried how Sensei caught jellyfish and prepared them, and how he kept a garden on the ship. Ziegfried listened with great interest but raised eyebrows.

"I don't think it's the best thing for you not to eat meat," he said.

"Sheba doesn't eat meat."

Ziegfried's face melted at the mention of her name. She was his queen.

"Sheba's not running herself into the ground fighting against the world."

"I'm not fighting against the world; I just don't want to kill animals anymore."

"Animals kill animals."

"I know."

"Humans have been eating animals for hundreds of thousands of years."

"I know."

"You're as stubborn as your grandfather."

"I feel fine."

"I stand corrected. You're *more* stubborn than your grandfather."

I smiled.

After our feast, Ziegfried pulled on the mask, which made him look like the Cyclops. He stepped into the water and carefully walked all around the sub, examining the hull, and occasionally taking a deep breath and sticking his head under water. I could tell by the stiffness of his movements how much he hated doing that. He tried to reach underneath the hull with his hands, feeling for barnacles and such, but had to go right under to see the keel and propeller. When he came out of the water he looked surprisingly happy for someone who liked being under water about as much as a cat.

"It's an amazing paint we put on her," he said, as he stood dripping into the sand. "But she needs to be repainted. You're probably losing four knots for all the barnacles you're carrying."

I shrugged. I didn't think it was that much. I could live with it anyway.

"She'll have to come out of the water." He looked me in the eye. I winced. Scraping and painting her was a huge job, and I knew who would be doing all the scraping.

"Where can we do that here?"

"We'll find a place. On an island like this there have to be good boathouses with pulleys for raising boats out of the water. We just have to find one to rent. We'll look in Naha."

I nodded. In spite of my resistance, I knew he was right. He always was. And I was incredibly grateful for what he was doing for me.

"I'm very sorry I broke our agreement. I just couldn't have lived with myself if I hadn't tried to rescue him."

Ziegfried shrugged and stared at the sea. I wished I knew what he was thinking. When he finally spoke, he surprised me.

"Agreements must be amended over time. You're a man, now, Alfred. I don't need to tell you what to do anymore. Truth is, I couldn't have lived with it either—if I were you. I was just trying to keep you alive, Buddy. That's *my* job, and it's not the easiest job in the world, I can tell you." Then he smiled and slapped me on the back. "Let's get her in shape, and get you back in the water."

Chapter Twenty-six

ᔈ

THE NEXT TIME we went to the hospital we found Sensei sitting up in bed, surrounded by family. He was pale and thin yet much improved, and smiling a lot. He looked different to me once again, dressed in a hospital gown and surrounded by people, young and old, who seemed to admire and respect him tremendously. Was this the ninja I had known on the ship? I hardly recognized him.

As it was already crowded in the little room, Ziegfried and I didn't want to intrude on a family gathering, but Sensei made an urgent gesture with his arms for me to come closer. So I did. But before I could reach the side of his bed, I had to shake hands with everyone in the room, because they wanted to thank me for rescuing him, which made me feel a little awkward. Everyone bowed also, which was customary in Japan. Ziegfried and I tried to imitate the bowing, and that was awkward too. Then in an act that made everyone in the room gasp, Sensei pulled his sword from the side of his bed, and held it out for me.

"This was my father's sword," he said. "I want you to have it. You are like a son to me."

I stared at the astonished looks on the faces of his family. This was a big deal, I knew, and I wasn't sure that everyone here agreed with it, especially one girl who was my age. She frowned at me. I didn't want to upset anyone by accepting the sword, but I couldn't insult Sensei by not accepting it. So I took it as gracefully as I could, bowed my head, and said that I would treasure it always and take good care of it.

"You will come to our home," said the next oldest man in the room, who must have been Sensei's brother. "We would be honoured if you would visit us when our dear brother is out of the hospital."

Ziegfried and I promised that we would. After a short chat with everyone, and an exchange of addresses, we were ushered out of the room by a very strict nurse. I never had a decent chance to speak with Sensei. The patient needs to rest, she said. Ziegfried and I shook Sensei's hand, bowed to everyone once again, and left the room. As we walked out of the hospital into the sunshine, I carried Sensei's sword proudly on my back.

"I bet that's sharp," Ziegfried said.

I remembered watching Sensei cut open a dead shark with the sword. "Yup," I answered. "It is."

∽

Naha was bustling compared to the quiet north of the island. And unlike Choshi it was colourful, full of shops, markets, and people. Newspapers and TV screens still showed pictures of the tsunami and the nuclear reactors at Fukushima, but people didn't wear masks, and didn't look frightened. People were unbelievably friendly, too.

Ziegfried said that Okinawa had the oldest population in the world, with more people over a hundred than anywhere else. That didn't surprise me. We saw lots of old people walking along the side of the road, tending gardens, or sitting outside their houses and waving as we went by, just as people did back in Newfoundland. It would have been so nice to travel all over the island, talking to people and exploring, but we had work to do.

Finding a boathouse to rent wasn't hard, but finding one with pulleys strong enough to lift the sub out of the water was. Communicating over the phone was tricky, too. Many people in the city spoke English, but once you went into the countryside, they didn't as much. On one of our searches, after confirming the exact dimensions of the boathouse and strength of the pulleys, we arrived at a small chicken farm.

The shed was a good size, and the pulleys were strong enough, but we were five miles from the sea.

It took two days to find the right one. The owner, a friendly, fast-talking businessman, was selling it, but was willing to rent it to us for three weeks. He was hoping we would buy it after that, but Ziegfried made it clear that wasn't a possibility.

Once we had the boathouse, we had to rent a boat. The boathouse was just north of an American military base near Naha. The only way to bring the sub in and out of the boathouse secretly was to sail it directly beneath a boat, with the top of the hatch nearly touching the bottom of the keel. Finding a suitable boat was almost as hard as finding the boathouse, unless we wanted to pay an insane amount of money to rent a fancy motorboat. Instead, we settled for an old fishing boat, which wasn't entirely sea-worthy, but which we were able to rent dirt-cheap because the old fisherman liked Ziegfried. Ziegfried loved Okinawa, and everyone he met here could feel that. He had half a mind to move here, he said, if he could talk Sheba into it. Good luck with that, I said.

Once we had arranged for the boat, Ziegfried moved out of his tiny cabin in Kunigami. We planned to work, eat, and sleep in the boathouse. It was the only way to get the work done and guarantee secrecy. I wasn't looking forward to three weeks of hard physical labour but kept that to myself. Ziegfried was doing me a great service, and I was grateful.

He, on the other hand, grew more cheerful with every tool we rented and every piece of material we bought—mostly second-hand. Ziegfried was as passionate about working with metal as I was about the sea. The only thing that excited him more was a big sprawling junkyard, which we found outside of Naha, and where I followed him around for three hours while he talked excitedly and waved his arms at all the uniquely Japanese junk. I had to resign myself once again to being his lackey, which, after being captain of my own vessel for almost three years, was a little humbling. Ziegfried said it was good for me to be humbled from time to time. It was character building.

∽

We moved the sub on a dark rainy night. We left the rented car at a fishing wharf on the south side of the island, just an hour's drive from Naha, and then spent the better part of the day motoring north in the fishing boat that Ziegfried described as "a washing machine in a bucket." The rain started in the afternoon. The boat coughed, shook, wheezed, and gasped for air until it reached six knots, its top speed. It was a long, slow trip, but Hollie and Seaweed seemed to enjoy it. And we did get a good look at the east coast of the island, even in the rain.

When we reached the north of the island and discovered the sub where we had left her, I was so relieved. I just wanted to crawl into my bed and have a good sleep. But Ziegfried said we had better continue around the point and down the

west side of the island while it was still dark. The less attention we drew to ourselves the better. So I made a pot of tea
and Ziegfried made a pot of coffee. He ploughed through
the waves for the rest of the night in the boat, and I followed
underneath in the sub. Hollie and Seaweed chose to stay on
the boat, where they knew they'd be spoiled with food and
attention. My only consolation was a large bag of candy I
had bought in Naha, which didn't have any iron or B12 in it
but sure kept my spirits up throughout the long night.

It took a lot of skill to stay right underneath the boat. It
helped that her engine was so rough, because I couldn't hear
it well enough to tell when she was pulling ahead, or dropping behind, or veering to port or starboard, but I could feel
the absence of her vibrations above my head. Whenever I
grew sleepy and didn't notice, I'd have to raise the periscope
and find her again. Once the sun was up, however, and we
sailed into the area north of Naha, where the American military base was, I had to stay alert. Not only was it necessary to
appear as one vessel on sonar and radar, the sub had to be
directly beneath the boat so that it would be invisible from
the air.

In truth, we weren't as afraid of being caught by the
American navy as we were by the Japanese coast guard. My
experience with the Americans had always been positive;
they did not consider me an outlaw. They might demand
that I sail on the surface within the three-mile zone, as required by international law, but they surely wouldn't see me

as a criminal in the way that Japanese authorities would.

We needn't have worried. From the water, the American base appeared just as quiet as everywhere else on Okinawa except Naha. By mid-morning we were sitting in front of the boathouse. I was absolutely exhausted. The last two hundred feet had been too shallow for the sub to stay beneath the fishing boat, so I had to drop behind, raise the periscope, and follow Ziegfried in, with the nose of the sub touching the stern of the boat. Once at the boathouse, Ziegfried jumped out, swung open the boathouse doors, and I glided the sub inside. We sealed the boathouse, and I went straight to bed. Ziegfried made another pot of coffee and motored the fishing boat all the way back to its cove, where he picked up the rental car, and drove back. I was dead to the world even before he left the boathouse.

Chapter Twenty-seven

◦✍◦

AFTER A GOOD LONG sleep I began my job as Ziegfried's lackey, which, truth be told, wasn't the most rewarding experience in the world. Ziegfried was one of the nicest people you could ever meet, that is, once you got to know him, but you wouldn't know it when he was working.

His mind was so focused on the task at hand that he would forget things like saying please and thank you when he asked me to pass him a tool, or fetch something. And if he looked at work I had done, such as filing clean a valve opening, or scraping off old paint, and it wasn't quite up to his standards, he'd tell me to do it over again in a cold, logical, scientific tone. If you were looking for encouragement, or a pat on the back, you wouldn't find it here, not now. This was a time for work.

After a whole morning of being ordered around like a slave, I was glad to lose myself for the rest of the day in the lonely scraping and sanding of the hull.

It was slow, tedious, muscle-aching work, but I kept telling myself how nice it would be to have the sub slicing through the water a few knots faster with a new coat of paint, or, well, five coats of paint. I remembered the barnacle skirt of Sensei's ship, how sluggish it was under sail, and that inspired me to stay at it.

Even though I couldn't hear terribly well, I had to wear earphones to block the screeching of the electric sander, because the vibrations would damage my ears. I also had to wear eye goggles and a face mask with special filters to protect my lungs from the toxic dust of the paint. Wrapped up in these protective masks, and wearing heavy cotton overalls and gloves, I sweated constantly. I had to stop every now and then to guzzle a bottle of water, and kept a bag of candy on the go to keep up my energy.

After five days without a break, except taking Hollie for walks, we received an invitation to Sensei's brother's house. We were invited for dinner. Thank Heavens! Not only was I relieved to get away from the boathouse for an evening, I was looking forward to seeing Sensei again.

The only problem was that we didn't have any clean

clothes. Neither did we have a shower or bathtub to wash up in. We were living in the boathouse day and night, cleaning ourselves in a bucket of fresh water, and shaking our clothes out in the wind. We simply couldn't afford the time to go to a laundromat, or wash our clothes by hand. We didn't realize how bad we actually stank until we stepped outside in the sunshine and examined each other.

I thought we were maybe passable, but Ziegfried said I had spent too much time at sea with a dog and a seagull, and could no longer tell the difference between dirty and clean. We couldn't visit Sensei's brother's home looking and smelling like two hoboes, he said. So we scrubbed extra hard with soap to get the dirt and grime off, spot-cleaned our clothes, and shook them out to dry. Then we inspected each other again.

"I hope I'm cleaner than you," Ziegfried said seriously.

"I don't think so," I said.

So we stopped at a department store on the way, bought two inexpensive pairs of pants, two pairs of socks, and two flowery shirts. Ziegfried said we'd be leaving our shoes outside anyway so we didn't have to buy new ones. For Ziegfried, we bought the largest pants and shirt they had, but the pants still only came halfway up his legs. He covered the rest of his hairy legs with long black socks that were meant for playing soccer. The only shirt that fit him was a stretchy one that pulled uncomfortably tight, and looked ready to burst. Ziegfried also bought a small bottle of cologne, which I thought was a terrible idea. He splashed the whole thing on both of us until we smelled like a flower shop. Although it was way too strong for my nose, Ziegfried said it was better than smelling like old stinky paint cans. I wasn't so sure.

Sensei's brother lived in a tidy wooden house that was rather plain but had a beautiful garden outside and a view of the sea. Sensei met us at the door and we exchanged bows and warm handshakes. I was so happy to see him. He looked much better. He introduced us to his family once again, and we met his great-grandnieces and nephews, including Himari, the girl who had frowned at me in the hospital.

I couldn't believe it was the same girl. She had long black hair, chestnut eyes, creamy skin, red lips, and long curled eyelashes. She wore a traditional Japanese dress over her lean curvy body. Standing in slippers, she was the same height as me. She was, to be honest, the most beautiful girl I had ever seen. As I reached out to take her hand, she said to me, "You saved my great-granduncle's life." And she bowed low.

It was the first time I understood the expression: "to have someone take your breath away." She did that to me.

Himari was very confident, if a little bossy. She seemed mature for her age, but was not much older than me. When she took a close look at us, I think she wanted to laugh. How I wished we had rented a hotel room to take a bath. At the very least I wished we hadn't bought the cheapest clothes in the store. There was nothing we could do about it now. Everyone looked at Ziegfried's socks and pants, and I was impressed that they never laughed.

For dinner we had sushi and rice with all sorts of fish and

vegetables in small dishes. Everything was tasty. I expected to see jellyfish, but there weren't any.

At first, the conversation was quiet, polite, and serious. Everyone spoke about the tsunami, the nuclear meltdown, and the terrible loss of life. But after a while the conversation grew animated, especially after Ziegfried, Sensei, and his brother drank sake, a drink with alcohol, which Ziegfried really liked, but I couldn't stomach. Himari sipped it slowly, which made me want to like it, but I just couldn't swallow it. I still couldn't understand why people liked alcohol. As far as my taste buds were concerned, it was just another fuel. You could light it with a match, and you could burn it in an engine.

I didn't want to be rude and stare at Himari, but she kept staring at me the whole time.

For dessert we had all sorts of extremely sweet rice cakes and cookies. I ate so many that I grew sleepy. I knew it wasn't polite to over-eat when you were invited for dinner, but Himari kept pushing the plates of cookies in front of me, and since I couldn't hear well enough to know what was making everyone else laugh so hard, I had nothing to do but eat. Ziegfried was sitting next to Sensei, and they were talking a lot, but I couldn't hear them.

After a while, Himari went to Sensei's seat to ask him something. She spoke into his good ear, and he nodded his head and smiled at me. Then she excused herself from the table, and gestured very politely for me to follow her, which

I did. She led me to a martial arts studio in the back of the house and asked me to wait there for a moment. I stood in the middle of the room, looking at the shiny steel swords on the wall. I saw dozens of wooden sticks in a large bucket and wire mesh masks hanging from hooks. This was a serious training studio. Himari returned wearing a white suit and black belt. She was talking excitedly now, though I couldn't hear every word. She pulled down two masks, handed one to me, and pulled out two wooden swords from the bucket. She tossed one towards me exactly the way Sensei would have. Unlike on the ship, I caught it. But did she intend to fight me? She pulled on her mask, so I did the same.

I didn't know what Sensei had told her about me, or why she would think I could fight, but she took an attack position and raised her wooden sword. The food in my stomach made loud gurgling noises. Oh boy.

I had never fought with a girl before and had been raised that you didn't hit girls, even if they hit you. I was taught that a man who struck a girl was a coward and a bully. This made a fight with Himari, even a wooden sword fight, tricky for me.

It wasn't tricky for her. She was obviously very used to fighting with boys, and she came at me as a warrior in full attack mode.

I was surprised to discover that just two weeks of intensive training with Sensei on the ship, during which I suffered more cuts, bruises, and sheer pain than at any other time in my life, had greatly sharpened my reflexes and ability to defend myself. So when Himari's stick swung through the air lightly and quickly, I met it with mine just in time to prevent it from hitting me. *Clack!* went the sticks. *Gurgle, gurgle,* went my belly.

I couldn't see her face through the mask, but I thought I heard her laugh. I wasn't sure. She swung again, and I blocked it. She twirled her whole body around in a movement I never saw Sensei make, and when her stick cut through the air it didn't come straight, it curved at the last second and struck me on the leg. It hurt, but I didn't show it. Now I had another dilemma: I didn't want her to think that I *couldn't* fight. She wouldn't respect me if she could beat the pants off me, and I did want her to respect me.

And so, I buckled down and focused very hard to defend myself. Himari came at me more and more aggressively without ever striking me a second time. I swung to defend myself, without ever intending to strike her. But I did.

She had backed me into a corner. She must have known I was purposefully trying not to hit her, and yet she kept attacking and attacking. One time when I swung back very hard to block her swing, my stick missed her stick and struck her on the side of her mask with a loud *whack!*

She stepped back. It must have hurt, and I wondered if it made her angry. She swung around in a circle twice, very quickly, like before. She was just a blur. When she came out of the spin, her stick was close to the ground. I jumped and it missed me. I was now in a perfect position to strike her on the mask again, and she knew it. But I didn't do it. I bent my knees instead and waited for her next strike. But it never came. She pulled off her mask. "Pretty good," she said. "Let's try something else."

We put the sticks and masks away. She stood in front of me and told me to grasp her arm firmly. So I did. She tugged at me, and I tugged back. Then she made a quick movement towards me, and the next thing I knew I was flying over her back and landing on the floor behind her. The gas in my belly came up my throat and out my mouth in one loud fast burp. It sounded exactly like a large pig.

"Excuse me," I said. I jumped to my feet. She was smiling and sweating, and looked very pleased. She was so beautiful. "I could teach you judo," she said.

"I think I'd like that."

She could have taught me how to clean out a sewer, and I would have liked it.

After a few more flips, and a kind of back and forth wrestling, which made me giddy, Himari wanted to show me her room, and another skill she was expert at—painting. She had an easel in front of the window, and the walls were covered with very skillful paintings of trees and birds and nature scenes. I was impressed. She kept talking, even though I couldn't hear every word. I just loved the sound of her voice. How nice it would be to learn Japanese, too. I was just beginning to wonder if Ziegfried was right about moving to Okinawa when he appeared at the door.

"Time to go, Buddy."

"Really?" It felt like we had just got here.

"I think you'll have to drive, Al. I've had too much sake."

"Okay."

Sensei's brother appeared at the door and insisted we stay over. That sounded pretty good to me but Ziegfried politely refused. We thanked our guests over and over, promising we would visit again as we climbed into the little car. Himari stood at the door with her elders and frowned. She didn't want me to go, and I didn't want to leave. I could still smell the sweet mix of her sweat and perfume, which was a world away from the cheap cologne we were wearing.

It was a sign of Ziegfried's confidence in me that he would ask me to drive the car back when I didn't have a license and had never driven on the left side of the road, as they do in Japan. But as it was a small city and late, there were almost no cars on the road. It didn't take me long to get the hang of it.

Ziegfried's fatigue had finally caught up with him. He fell asleep after only ten minutes in the car. I had a hard time waking him when we got back. He staggered into the boathouse, flopped down on his sleeping mat, and went to sleep for twelve hours. I climbed into the sub with Hollie, fed him, tried to wash off the cologne, brushed my teeth, and dropped onto my cot with a smile. I couldn't stop thinking of Himari.

Chapter Twenty-eight

FOR THE NEXT TWO weeks we worked hard refitting the sub, and didn't often leave the boathouse. I spent so much time wrapped up in goggles and masks that I felt like a spaceman. Fortunately there was always a good breeze, and we left the windows open for fresh air, although we had to hang make-shift curtains so that people couldn't see inside. Although few people ever came close enough, we were extra careful. All it would take would be one person to see the sub, recognize Hollie and me from news footage a few months earlier, and call the police. However unlikely that might be, we just couldn't take the risk.

If we needed something, Ziegfried usually went into town

alone and I stayed in the boathouse. But sometimes we did go together so I could help search for hoses, valves, pipes, nuts and bolts, or whatever was needed. While we could have bought those things new, they cost next to nothing at the junkyard; it only made sense to save as much money as possible, especially when the paint was expensive. Ziegfried had found a supplier for the paint in Naha, and had cut a deal for it, something he was expert at doing.

The few times we did go into the city together we picked up food items to restock the sub for the trip across the Pacific. I was planning to stop in Saipan, where I had been before and knew people. I could refuel there and restock with fresh fruit and vegetables. Still, as Saipan was fifteen hundred miles away, Ziegfried insisted we restock as much of the dried and canned food as possible. You never know when you might have to leave in a hurry, he said.

Once I had finished scraping, belt-sanding, and preparing the outside hull for painting, and once we had applied the primer, there was nothing more for me to do until it dried, which would take two days before we could begin repainting. For the first few hours we couldn't even stay in the boathouse; it was too toxic. So we lay down on the grass outside, stared up at the clouds and rested. I took the chance to suggest that maybe we could visit Sensei again, as Himari had offered to teach me judo, which I thought would be an important skill to learn.

Staring up at the clouds and chewing on a piece of dry grass, Ziegfried said, "Judo?"

"Yes. It's excellent self-defence. It could come in really handy, you know, if I were ever attacked again. I've been attacked before, you know?"

"By who? Himari?"

"No. I was attacked by a pirate in South Africa."

"That's terrible, Al. And you feel that if you knew judo you could have better defended yourself?"

"Yes, I think so."

"Well, that's something to think about. Maybe when you get back to Newfoundland we can find you a teacher of judo."

"In Bonavista Bay?"

"Yeah, you never know."

"I was wondering if maybe I should hang around here a bit longer so that I could learn from Himari."

"Oh. I see. I suppose she could also teach you how to paint."

The thought had occurred to me. "That wouldn't be such a bad idea. That would give me something to do during the long stretches at sea."

"I don't know, Al. I'd kind of wonder if you'd ever leave once you started taking lessons from her."

"Of course I would."

"The truth is, Al, you've got to get to sea as soon as that last coat of paint is dry."

"Really? Why?"

"Are you forgetting that you're a wanted man, Al, here and in Australia? You're enjoying a sense of freedom right now because I'm here, and because the tsunami and nuclear meltdown have required many local police to go to the mainland to help out. Once they come back, and once I'm gone, the chances of your getting stopped and questioned go up one thousand percent. And that's all it would take— one questioning by an officer, who would immediately realize you're not here legally. And once they figure out who you are . . . Make no mistake about it, Al, you'd be playing a dangerous game. You wouldn't be the first man to spend a lifetime in prison after enjoying a few weeks with a lovely girl."

Ziegfried had such a way of putting things sometimes.

"I guess so."

"There are lots of pretty girls in Newfoundland, too, you know."

"Yeah." I had never seen anyone like Himari in Newfoundland, and I didn't feel like looking.

"If you like her so much, why don't you invite her to come visit us there?"

"Really? Do you think I could?"

"I don't see why not. I bet a girl like that would really enjoy such a trip. I know Sheba would love to have her. And then you could learn all the judo and painting you want."

"That sounds pretty good. I wonder if she'd come."

"Only one way to find out. For now, Al, let's just focus on getting you back in the water as quickly as we can, okay?"

"Okay."

Ziegfried's words were more accurate than I could have imagined. Within a few days we started to notice more police presence on the waterfront. It felt almost as though they were looking for me, but that was just my nervousness about getting caught, Ziegfried said. Stay calm, stay out of sight, and get the work done. The only problem with that was that it prevented us from making another trip to visit Sensei and Himari. It didn't, however, prevent them from visiting us, although they came when we least expected it, and not exactly at the best time.

As I've said, when you work in the same clothes day after day you get pretty stinky, especially if you're sweating a lot. We couldn't help it. Okinawa has a very warm climate, yet we couldn't work in shorts and t-shirts; we had to keep our skin covered. Every day it was our intention to clean our clothes, or at least clean our spare clothes that were lying in a heap in the corner of the boathouse for over a week, but there was always some pressing issue, some work that had to be done right away, and the washing kept being put off. Each day started out with us declaring that we would do it, and each day ended with us having forgotten. Ziegfried said that Sheba would be horrified at the sight of us. I said I was glad that Himari couldn't see us either. That's when Ziegfried said, "She's outside, Al."

I laughed. I thought he was joking.

"Pat down your hair, Al. It's sticking up; you look like a porcupine."

I turned and looked at Ziegfried. He looked like a character from an old silent movie, like a giant version of Charlie Chaplin who had just destroyed a bakery by accident, bringing all the flour, dust, and dough on top of himself. His face was pasty white, and his teeth looked black. When he removed his goggles there were two dark rings around his eyes, like a raccoon's. I couldn't tell what he smelled like because everything smelled the same to me . . . bad.

There was a knock at the door.

"You'd better get it, Al," Ziegfried said as he bent down to stick his head into the only clean bucket of water, and washed his face really quickly.

I went and opened the door. Standing there, as fresh and clean as a spring flower, was Himari. Beside her were two old Japanese men looking neat and tidy: Sensei and his brother. I bowed low immediately, as was customary in Japan when meeting highly respected elders. The irony of the difference between this meeting and my first one with Sensei was not lost on me, but I was glad to see him strong on his feet, and more than happy to show him respect.

I wasn't sure they actually recognized us at first. Ziegfried came over looking like a bear with dripping fur. He had stuck his head right inside the bucket, and then wiped his face dry with the corner of the shirt he had bought at the store, which had slowly been morphing into a grease rag. He also bowed low to the old men. We had, in fact, practised bowing properly, the way they do it in Japan, which is not just a drop of the head but a whole movement of the back. The more respect you wanted to show, the lower you bowed.

"We had to come and visit you," Himari said. "I wanted to see your submarine. My great-granduncle has said you have travelled all over the world in it. Is it true?"

I nodded. "I'm afraid we have been working so much we haven't been able to clean up much." They were probably starting to think we were always like this.

Himari smiled and stepped carefully into the boathouse. When she saw the sub hanging in the air, all shiny and new-looking with three coats of paint, her eyes opened wide. "Wow! It is amazing!"

"Yeah, it's pretty cool, I guess," I said.

Sensei and his brother stepped just inside the open doors, and Sensei spoke excitedly to him in Japanese, pointing to the sub and gesturing wildly. I wondered what he was saying. I wondered if his family had any idea just how remarkable he had been out at sea. I wanted to tell them, but I never seemed to get the chance.

"Can I look inside?" Himari asked.

"Um . . . sure. You might have trouble getting in though."

She didn't. She reached up to a handle high above her head, and pulled herself up. She was strong. I half expected to see Sensei do the same thing, but he was being careful with his healing lung. He smiled a lot, although I couldn't help thinking he was concealing a deep desire to be back at sea. "When will you go back to sea?" he asked me.

"As soon as the last coat of paint is dry," I answered. "Two more coats." Then I wondered out loud, "And you? Will you buy another ship?"

Sensei kept smiling but his eyes betrayed his deep disappointment. "I have no money for a ship," he said. "Will I go to sea? I don't know. I would like to continue to clean up plastic. But the doctor says I must stay on land now, at my brother's house. I don't know; I will think about it. My great-grandniece would like me to teach ninjutsu. I think I would like that very much, too."

"I wish I could stay to learn it from you," I said.

"You are a good student," he said. "But the sea needs you more than the land does. There are many people dedicated to saving the land. Not so many for the sea, I think. You are a ninja of the sea, like the seals and the gulls. It makes my heart glad knowing you will be out there, caring for it."

"I will do my best," I said.

"I know that you will. You do not know how to *give up*." And he smiled widely, and his eyes watered.

I knew then that his sailing days were over.

Chapter Twenty-nine

WHEN THE POLICE car cruised by I was inside the sub with Himari. I had climbed in to see what was taking her so long. I found her in the bow, on the floor. She had drawn Sensei's sword from its sheath, and was studying the markings on the blade. I couldn't help feeling badly; I thought Sensei should have given it to her, not me. She thought so too.

The boathouse side doors were wide open when the police car pulled up. I heard car doors shut and someone speaking Japanese with a sharp tone. I peeked through the periscope. Two Japanese officers were standing next to Ziegfried, staring intensely at the sub.

"Yes," said Ziegfried loudly, "it is *my* submarine." He nodded towards Sensei. "He inspired me to build it." The officers exchanged bows with Sensei and his brother. "Yes," Ziegfried said, "it will have to be tested . . . No, we do not have its papers yet . . . No, it has not been in the water yet . . . No, there is no one inside . . . Yes, that is my dog . . . Yes, my passport is around here, somewhere . . . "

Ziegfried dug through his bag and found his passport. The police officers studied it and gave it back. Then they wanted to see his plane ticket. They *took* it! They were growing more suspicious. They kept asking the same questions over and over.

"No, there is no one inside the submarine," Ziegfried said again loudly, and I knew he was warning me. "You want to look inside? Okay, but I am *sure* you won't find anyone inside."

I took Himari by the hand. There was only one place to hide. In the cold room in the stern there was a spot where we could pull up the floor. While it gave access to the crankshaft, it wasn't really meant for crawling inside. I could fit, but Ziegfried couldn't. The opening was beneath boxes of canned food. I felt the sub tilt slightly as one of the officers grabbed hold of an outside handle. They were coming up!

Himari followed me quickly into the cold room and I gently pulled the door shut. Then I slid the boxes away. There was no handle on the floor. You had to fit your fingers between the floorboards, push down on one side, and pull up on the other. Then you could lift it up. There really wasn't enough room for two people. But that's where we went.

"Are you claustrophobic?" I whispered.

She shook her head, and climbed inside. I followed, and pulled the floorboards down on top of us.

Himari was wearing a white skirt and a light green blouse, but she squeezed into the greasy pit without hesitating. As our bodies pressed together like two sardines in a can—which was pretty much what I smelled like—I felt the second officer climb onto the hull.

The only light was what came from under the floor from the engine compartment. We couldn't hear anything because there was a steel wall between the stern and the rest of the sub, to prevent water from passing through. I could feel Himari's breath on my neck. If she was feeling fear or anxiety, she never showed it. We lay there together for a long time and just waited.

It was nerve-wracking, hot, and the air was going stale quickly. I couldn't help thinking of what Sensei must have suffered in the belly of the ship. I could barely turn my head, but when I did, I saw Himari's eyes staring at me, inches away.

"I'm sorry," I whispered.

"It's okay."

"I'm sorry that I stink."

"My great-granduncle told me that it is the stink of a noble young man," she said, and giggled quietly.

That made me smile. "I think he should have given his sword to you."

"You have to earn it," she said. "You did. I didn't."

"I think you are earning it right now." We both giggled. Suddenly the door swung open and light flooded into the tiny room above us. Two feet came in and stood right over our heads, no more than four inches away. With the light came a stream of fresh air. I breathed it silently into my lungs. I felt Himari's hand press against my hand. Was she holding my hand?

It felt like forever that the man stood above us and spoke to his partner in the bow. They spoke rapidly in Japanese. I wished I could have understood it. I felt Himari's breath on my neck, and it tingled through my body like a bolt of electricity. I felt it in my toes.

Finally we felt the men climb the portal and make their way down to the deck of the boathouse. They didn't bother to seal the door to the cold room. Once they were back on the ground, they continued interrogating Ziegfried. They didn't sound satisfied with his answers.

"What's that?" Ziegfried said loudly. "I'm sorry. I'm speaking loudly because the electric sanders have damaged my hearing. It's the nature of the work I do . . . Yes, I build submarines for a living . . . Yes, I am sure that is my dog . . . When will I be finished? Oh . . . in a few months I suppose . . . Yes, we will have papers . . . Yes, legal papers . . . You will come back? Okay. When? . . . When will you come back? . . . This evening? With coast guard? Okay. That is very good. I will be happy to show my submarine to the coast guard . . . Yes. Thank you. Thank you. You're welcome. Bye for now."

Ziegfried's voice grew more distant, and I knew they had moved outside. One part of me wanted to climb out and let Himari out, but another part of me wanted to keep feeling her breath on my neck.

Eventually I felt a much heavier weight tug on the hull outside, and I knew that Ziegfried was climbing up. "Coast is clear, Al. You'd better come out quick."

I pushed up the floorboards, climbed out, and reached down to help Himari out. Like me, she was covered in sweat and grease.

"That was brave of you," I said.

She smiled. "Did I earn my great-granduncle's sword?"

"I certainly think so. But how can I give it to you without insulting him?"

"I can hide it from him."

"I don't know." I didn't like the sound of that.

"Al! Quick! Let's go!"

"Okay."

So we climbed out and down to the deck. Ziegfried was already unlocking the pulleys to lower the sub into the water. "Quick, Al, grab the other ones."

"What are we doing?"

"*We* are getting *you* ready. You are leaving."

"I am?"

"You are."

The sub fell into the water with a splash.

"They'll be back in a few hours, Al, with the coast guard. They'll know the difference then. Grab the water!" He pointed to the large fresh water jugs.

"What about fuel?"

"You've got enough to make it to Saipan. Don't forget you can pedal."

"I won't. But what about your plane ticket? They took it. How will *you* get away?"

"It's all arranged, Al. Sensei arranged a spot for me on a private ferry to the mainland. Back-up plan. Grab those tools! Just throw them inside. You can sort them out later."

"But . . . what if they search for you on the ferry?"

"I'll be long gone before they ever think of it, Al. Grab those foodstuffs. Here, take these tools. You should have enough food to last you a few weeks. Good Heavens, don't forget Hollie. Here!"

He passed me Hollie and I carried him inside. I couldn't believe we were leaving like this. It was a mess inside. Every compartment was open. My foodstuffs were mostly in burlap sacks in the corners. My cot was on its side. "Is everything ready to go?" I yelled out.

"Well, we only got three coats on her but at least it's dry. The engine's ready. The electrical is hooked up. The crankshaft is clear. The plumbing's done. She should be good enough to sail. Island hop as much as you can. Stop in Saipan. Stop in Hawaii. Anywhere else you can. Double-check all your systems once you're at sea. Where's Seaweed? Can you call your first mate, Al?"

I grabbed a bag of dog biscuits, shook them, and called for Seaweed. It took a few minutes but he flew inside the boat-house, landed on the hatch, and jumped inside. I shut the hatch to make sure he stayed in, and climbed back to the deck. Himari was standing stiffly next to Sensei and his brother. I wondered if she had hurt herself in the sub.

I bowed low, and thanked them for all their help. Sensei had small tears in his eyes, but he smiled boldly and shook my hand vigorously.

"You are like my own son."

"I am honoured to hear that," I said. "I will write to you."

"Come on, Al."

"Okay." I shook hands with Sensei's brother. Then I stood in front of Himari. "Will you visit me in Canada?" I asked.

"I would love to. Write to me."

"I will."

We hugged each other. She was definitely stiff. I hoped she was okay.

"I will take a bath before you visit," I said.

"Take more than one." She smiled.

"Al . . ."

"Okay."

Ziegfried gave me one of his great bear hugs. "Al, I have an uncle on Vancouver Island. He's got a terrific boathouse. Why don't you sail there and we will meet you. Sheba would love it."

"Vancouver Island?"

"Yes. Why not? Call me on the shortwave when you get close, and we will come out. Okay?"

"Ahh . . . okay."

"Good. Go now. Do what you do best: sneak out of this place."

"I love you all," I said, and jumped onto the hull, opened the hatch, and climbed inside. I sealed the hatch, let water into the tanks, engaged the batteries, and quietly motored out of the boathouse. It was the middle of the afternoon. I took one last look through the periscope and saw all four of them climb into the same car and drive away. They weren't wasting any time.

As the sub sliced through the water as silently as a moth, I stood at the sonar panel and watched us dive until we reached three hundred feet. Once we were there I let a little air into the tanks to create neutral buoyancy. How much more enjoyable it was to do that in a submarine. I turned to pick up Sensei's sword, to see the writing on the blade that Himari had been reading. But it wasn't there. That was strange. I scoured the entire sub, and couldn't find it. Then it hit me: she had taken it. That's why she had been standing so stiffly —she was hiding the sword in her skirt. I had to laugh: how like a ninja. Like great-granduncle, like great-grandniece.

Rightly so that she should have taken it, I thought; it was her heritage, not mine. Besides, I wouldn't need a steel blade to remember Sensei.

Hours later, safely outside of Japanese waters, we rose to the surface and I opened the hatch. Fresh air rushed in, but I could still feel Himari's breath on my neck and still smell the fragrance of her. She hadn't taken only the sword; she had taken my heart.

Epilogue

⁓

ONCE MORE WE sailed over the waters where Sensei's ship had gone down, or very close to it. I never tried to look for her; I knew she was down there. She would have found a spot in darkness and silence—a place of the sea's own keeping. The sea was a jealous keeper of secrets.

I wondered if the plastic in her holds would stay there for a thousand years. What would archaeologists think if they found it? Would plastic be an ancient artifact by then, just another example of our peculiar habit of creating things that turn around and harm us?

Or will we have destroyed ourselves by then, and the

planet, too? Will the ship be discovered in a million years by aliens, who will think that plastic must have been so valuable as to have been sealed up inside a ship, like a treasure?

I had come to Japan to see if the hearts of whalers could be changed towards the most gentle creatures of the sea. Instead, I met a man who had spent one half of his life spreading plastic all over the world, and the rest picking it up. In a way, that answered my question. If one man's heart could change so completely, then anyone's could. These were the thoughts I had as we sailed two miles above his ship.

And one more: Sensei was living his last years in the company of loving family, on the island where he was born. He wasn't lying dead in the belly of the ship below us. For this I felt immensely grateful. It filled me with hope—hope that we could triumph over all the forces that threatened the sea, no matter how strong they were.

I climbed the portal with Hollie, and we leaned against the hatch as the stars began to appear. Seaweed rode on the hull below us, shaking his beak in the spray. The Pacific lay ahead of us so wide and infinite it was hard to believe it could ever die.

"We will save it, Hollie," I said as I leaned down and nuzzled his furry forehead with my face. "We will save it because we will never give up."

ABOUT THE AUTHOR

Philip Roy divides his time between two places with his family, and their Wonder Cat, Ollie: his hometown of Antigonish, Nova Scotia, and his adopted town of Durham, Ontario. Continuing to write adventurous and historical children's novels focusing on social, environmental and global concerns, Philip is also delighted to be embarking upon a new novel with Ronsdale Press, *The Kingdom of No Worries*, due out in the fall of 2017. He also looks forward to having his *Happy the Pocket Mouse* series translated into French. Along with writing, travelling, running, composing music, and crafting folk art out of recycled materials, Philip spends his time with his family. Visit Philip at www.philiproy.ca.

More Adventures with Alfred & His Submarine

PHILIP ROY

- **Submarine Outlaw**
  978-1-55380-058-3 PRINT
  978-1-55380-145-0 E-BOOK

- **Journey to Atlantis**
  978-1-55380-076-7 PRINT
  978-1-55380-074-3 E-BOOK

- **River Odyssey**
  978-1-55380-105-4 PRINT
  978-1-55380-117-7 E-BOOK

- **Ghosts of the Pacific**
  978-1-55380-130-6 PRINT
  978-1-55380-136-8 E-BOOK

- **Outlaw in India**
  978-1-55380-177-1 PRINT
  978-1-55380-178-8 E-BOOK

- **Seas of South Africa**
  978-1-55380-247-1 PRINT
  978-1-55380-248-8 E-BOOK

- **Eco Warrior**
  978-1-55380-347-8 PRINT
  978-1-55380-348-5 E-BOOK

MARQUIS

Québec, Canada